SPIRITED OBSESSION

JUMOKE OKUWOBI

Spirited Obsession

ISBN: 979 – 871-294-523-8

Published by Hundred Hues Limited

Cover Illustration by @Onegraphiks

Edited by Tunde Aiyegbusi.

Also By Jumoke Okuwobi

A Ration of Thorns

ticks of the two clocks. He had not moved an inch, even to go to her lest the situation became real. He seemed to be strangely comforted by the silence after all the shouting, which the walls and corridor were used to.

He willed himself to his feet, nervously pulling at his tie which seemed to be too suffocating as he tried to swallow lumps of breath that did not want to go down. He then reached into the breast pocket of his jacket for his mobile phone to call someone. Looking into the blank screen which came to life, her stern face emerged on the screen and for a moment or two, he froze midway to unlocking the phone. Her picture was his screen saver and was also the background picture on his phone. A surge of anger ripped through him and the urge to smash the phone was overwhelming. Just then the email notification popped up with emails from work, a clear reminder of his obligations to work soon quelled his anger by reminding him of his responsibilities. But all these thoughts soon faded from his mind as he contemplated the matter again. Although a part of him wished to go down the stairway to check on her, another part of him wondered as to why it was not his first instinct to go after her as she tumbled and came to a final stop. And there she laid in that awkward angle, his wife, the Rapturer. Was it possible to hate someone so much even with their death? He must act. Once again his attention was turned to the phone which he had lowered to his side. Gently and with a steady hand, he raised it up again, surprised at how steady it was. Almost immediately, it began to ring and it was his friend Patrick. With a sinking heart reality set in at a rushed pace, as his obligations, responsibilities, meetings and reputation all at once came as multiple reminders of who he was. There was a board meeting holding within the hour and he could not miss his presentation to the board members.

His presentation from his committee was a crucial one. It was going to seal his nomination to the highest rank in the organization. He sighed wearily, suddenly tired of everything. Now life and purpose had all gone to waste and everything was about to crash.

He answered the phone.

'Hello Patrick' he said quietly

'Toks where are you now?' The urgency in the voice was compelling.

'I am at home, he hesitated.

'Something has happened.

Chapter 1

Back then in 1990 I had just gained admission into the Imperial College Business School in London. I was in my second year of Engineering, finally and happily enjoying the company and comfort of peers; free from my father's constant reminder that I was an underachiever unlike my elder sister, Tinuke, the Lawyer. I was not a very bright student when I was in secondary school and I had struggled with my studies. He was often criticizing and intimidating me. My father, Oriyomi Taylor, was a diplomat to the United Kingdom and for the past two years while he was away, I was free from his strict and firm parenting. I was finally happy and doing very well in the engineering course that I had chosen to study. But that was not good enough for my father and he had insisted I sat for foreign exams. My old man had pulled all the strings he could in ensuring that I got a place at the Imperial College in London. I had thought I was finally going to be my own person and yet I was dragged into his stronghold. He wielded a tremendous amount of influence on me. He was a man who fancied himself as elite from a fine line of Lagos aristocrats. Nothing was good enough for that man.

As soon as I got my letter of admission for the Business School of Imperial College my heart sank. It was not because I was not happy about the admission but it felt like a noose had been strapped over my neck and I was powerless against its gradual tightening. I had actually performed well at the exams. My best friend, Patrick had been enthusiastic. We had both grown up in the same environment and our lives have been intertwined. Patrick was the brother I never had. He was a friend who knew how frustrated I was by the total control my father had over me. We met ten years ago when I was about eight years old. We had just moved into our Ikoyi home in Lagos and I was excited about the ample back yard with its big lawn, trees and shrubs that lined the low fenced wall that separated our compound from the next house. I had been riding my bicycle and was a little bored because my sister and mother had gone to the market for some grocery shopping. My sister was much older than I was by seven years.

It had been a wet afternoon and the rains had just stopped, the cloudy weather was beginning to give way to a sunny one. Riding my bicycle gave me such a sense of excitement and circling that ample yard was one of life's pleasures for me at my age. I stopped when I thought that I heard a noise from the tree that leaned against the fence. But then all was quiet again and I began to peddle in a circular motion. Suddenly, a pebble hit me right in the face and I immediately stopped peddling and looked towards the angle from which the offending stone had emerged. It was a boy about my age, perched on the tree and he was grinning as though he had won a prize. He jumped down from the tree like an accomplished gymnast and walked towards me as though it was the most natural thing to do. He was the same height as me, and was wearing a blue tee shirt and brown khaki shorts. He walked with a self-assured swagger like the American kids on television and he came forward without any introduction. I sat astride on my bicycle and watched him approach without a word and waited for this brave stranger.

'Nice bike' he said without taking his eyes off the bicycle.

'Can I ride it?' He asked. Without waiting for a reply, began to hold onto the handle of the bike.

'Hold on' I said to him

'Who are you? My father might not be happy to see you riding this' I said looking towards the house in trepidation. But the boy ignored my protestations and gently but firmly took control of the bike. He rode awkwardly at first but he had such a confidence about him that masked his ineptitude.

At that age and period of my life, I was so impressionable and easily intimidated, a fault my father never failed to point out. One would have thought that being his only son he would cut me some slack but the man was very hard on me and I was fearful of him as against loving him the way a father and son would bond. I allowed Patrick access to my bike that afternoon even though I really did not want him riding it. After all, I did not know him. But his self – assuredness and charming manner disarmed me. We became friends that afternoon.

We had taken our common entrance examinations and had attended the prestigious Kings College Lagos for our secondary education. We both sat for the WAEC (West African Examination Commission and the JAMB Joint Admissions Matriculations Board examination) and gained admission to the University of Lagos at the same time. We were like Siamese twins. And now at eighteen and preparing to join the league of 'club boys on campus, a social club with its own league of big and influential boys on campus. I was pretty excited about it and the parties would elevate me into the school's big boys, Patrick's words. The club boys were an elitist group of rich boys who either came from rich homes or had proven themselves worthy with material possessions ranging from cars to expensive jewelry and clothing. The party for this was slated for the weekend. I had a troubling feeling that my father could summon me at any point in time and I was worried that I would miss the induction ceremony. Those were my concerns as a young adult then, but I did not know that the course of my life was about to change. On that Friday night of the induction party, with still no word from father or summons to come home, I happily remained on campus and was looking forward to the club party that I was going to attend that night.

The University of Lagos was like a haven for me. I particularly enjoyed the environment, the freedom and the various campus activities. I was living in the boys' quarters at the senior staff residence and it was my first time of staying away on my own away from any parental guidance, especially the strict watchful eyes of my father. I never attended boarding school.

All day long Patrick and I had talked about how we would score with the 'happening babes' that were sure to show up and we had been grooming ourselves for most part of the day. That night, I had my first smoke of marijuana. Patrick with whom I was sharing the room with and some of the other big boys who were referred to as staff quarter's boys, had brought in the joint to my room. I did not particularly care for it but I had to behave as though I was ok with it. It was also a night that I first fell in love and felt untouchable. After taking some drags of the joint, we set off for the party. By the time we arrived it had been on its way with dancing and some choreographic performances, rap lip syncs and girls making eyes at the guys. There was a lot of drinking and hardly anything to eat and I was beginning to feel hungry.

I was having the time of my life when she walked in with

some of her friends. She was breath taking and for the longest moment I could not take my eyes off her. I knew without a doubt that I would somehow make a connection with this goddess. She was simply different; everyone was dressed in the latest hip hop outfit. She wore a simple black half cropped tee shirt and a black pair of baggy jeans. She stood out in a way that was captivating and alluring to me. Her hair was packed into a tight bun and the freshness of her face was almost a platitude of sheer innocence. I was blown away by her looks. I was mesmerized as I watched her. I also watched as guy after guy approached her and she turned them down. Patrick soon came up to me and I asked him if he knew her or her friends.

'Oh those ones are the 'freshers' he said dismissively of the new undergrads.

Their drama is too much.'

'There are other girls here' he said pointing with his glass cup to another set of girls who were making eyes at us in another corner of the hall. As he pointed out other girls to me I could not seem to pull my eyes off her. I saw that she darted glances every now and then to me and shifted uncomfortably in her seat and whispered with her friends.

'I am going for her' I said with a confidence that I did not know I had.

'Well it's your prerogative' Patrick said slapping me on the shoulder in compliance with the music 'My prerogative' by Bobby Brown that was blaring from the speakers behind us.

I summon up the courage to approach her and I said the first thing that came out of my head.

'Do you think you can dance to this?' She smiled at me and nodded shyly.

I took her hand and lead her to the dance floor. I took a quick look at Patrick who appeared as if he could not believe what was happening. Whether it was the effect of the Marijuana I had tried earlier or the overwhelming presence of this girl I could not tell, I suddenly felt fearless and a surge of manliness came over me wanting only to protect and hold on to this beautiful stranger. I was dancing like I had never danced in my life simply to impress her. Just as I thought I could do no more justice to the music, the deejay changed it to a slow rhythm and blues number and my heart sank. Most of the girls I knew only danced to slow numbers with their boyfriends or someone that they were surely intimate with and I was afraid that I was going to be denied of her company too soon. But she smiled at me invitingly and I had no choice than to open up my arms, which she stepped into without hesitation.

I was on cloud nine as our bodies merged into one and we began to sway to the slow rhythm. I felt the need to protect and enfold this girl like I had never felt for anyone in my life. I gently smelt her as we moved and her perfume intoxicated me further. I felt enraptured and gave in to the sweet surrender of her power. I hoped that she would not notice my hardness as I tried but failed to hide my arousal during the dance. If she minded I did not know because she said nothing and held onto my neck with her fingers entwined. When I could find my voice I asked for her name.

'Omolola Bailey"

For a moment I was happy that she was Yoruba like me. And I told her my name.

"I am Tokunbo Taylor"

'Yes I know' she said, raising her face to look at the puzzlement on my face.

'Everyone knows who you are' she declared.

I stopped moving and we locked eyes for the longest moment in that dimly lit hall oblivious to everything and everyone. It was as though we had a special language that was exclusively ours. There were so many questions I wanted to ask her, like who she was, and where she had come from but most importantly could she be mine? There was a certain quality about her that drew me to her and I could not place nor articulate even to myself.

We began to move again this time prompted by her with eyes still locked in that magnetic embrace.

Soon enough, the music changed and the lights which were dimmed earlier lit up the room and couples soon broke off their locked bodies. I was sorry to let go but I was not yet done with her and I managed to steer her out of the dance hall.

As we walked into the darkness outside, I gently led her away from the hall towards a pathway that led to a clearing, just before the water front of the university. Soon enough, I began to sense her apprehension and I reassured her that it was alright. I knew of a particular clearing that lead to the driveway with street lights and this reassured her. We walked and talked for hours that night and I got to know so much about her. I revealed myself to her like I had never done with anyone before. I wanted her to know me more. As she also spoke, I fell for her even harder. The only thing I left out was my impending departure from the University. She told me that she was a law student and was from Lagos state like I was. The Bailey's were an old Lagos family like mine.

As we continued our midnight stroll along the water front, the moon illuminated our pathway and gave off a slivery gleam on the lagoon. It added to the magical mystery of the night. More often than not, we encountered other couples walking and whispering and some locked in passionate embraces, a confirmation of our own mission. At some point, our fingers found each other and they remained entwined. I could not get enough of Omolola that night. She was a head shorter than I was and she had such expressive eyes that could put a man at ease. I was completely besotted.

She was lively and animated as she spoke about her feelings, her hopes and aspirations for the future. I had never encountered anyone who was as passionate about the law as she was. She had a formidable intellect. I wanted to have her there and then but I knew that that would be moving too fast, I was sad that I would not have that time if and when I would be shipped off to London. But I continued to savor the moment knowing that I would remember the present for all time. I was already in love with this beauty. We soon found ourselves by the dorms and I was reluctant when I had to let her go. We had talked and walked for miles it seemed not knowing where and when the time had passed. I wanted to leave her with something to remember me by but I had nothing on me and money would have been insulting. So I asked her what perfume she had on and she told me it was called 'Obsession.' I then asked her to promise me that she would always wear it. And she smiled and nodded as though she were agreeing to a proposal from me. Just as we were parted, I called her back and gave her my watch. I was reluctant to let go of her hand and she in turn surprised me. I had imagined kissing her all through our walk and without

I sighed wearily as I rose to follow Mr. John, it was as though I were walking towards the hangman's noose.

He was seated comfortably like royalty when I entered the living room of the Professor who was my guardian on campus. I proceeded to prostrate in greeting before both of them as tradition and custom demanded.

My father reveled in such flagrant display of custom and he had often longed for a chieftaincy title. Which sooner or later he might just buy or be conferred with since everyone and anyone was being given any native title. I scrambled up and waited for the sentence.

'So like I was saying,' he said turning to the Professor, after acknowledging my greetings 'he has gained admission to study business finance at the Imperial College and we have to leave tonight for London.'

As soon as he said that my heart sank and all I could think of was Omolola. I could picture her in my mind waiting at the banks of the Lagoon.

I stood silently listening to the two men talk about how fortunate I was to have gained admission to such a world - class institution.

'Although I would have preferred Oxford of course' my father said motioning at me by bringing me back to their discussion and I seethed inside with rage at the imposition of his choices on my life. I wanted to be heard and not this incapable child that he thought I was and also because I felt the only way to survive Nigeria was to school here and probably have my masters abroad. I knew that the level of education was declining but my childish idea was that there was no reason to study about foreign economies and try to apply them to our domestic one without having a thorough background on how ours work. Besides I actually enjoyed the engineering course I was already pursuing but I knew even that was not good enough for him. But he was my father and he knew the world better than I did. After all he was a diplomat. And as usual I stood dumb struck at his presence quietly waiting for his next command. They began to talk about the Military government and some of the injustices the masses especially, the lecturers in the tertiary institutions, were experiencing. As far as my father was concerned, the Military situation in the country was unsuitable for his family to be in and hence his resolve to relocate every member of his household to the United Kingdom. That resolution became urgent after the failed Military coup of the 22nd of April 1990. I continued to stand in silence, I thought of Patrick and our friendship. I had not focused on this separation because somehow I always believed that he and I would always and must surely be together, especially since he had a close rapport with my father. His uncle, our neighbor, Chief Diete-Spiff could afford to send him to London too but it did not seem to be happening. And now it seemed as though I would be abandoning him too.

Perhaps there was something I could say to my father? Knowing him like I did he would shoot down that dream as he had crushed other dreams of mine. He often told me how privileged I was to have a father like him to provide me with a good education and the many comforts of life that I enjoyed. Unlike him he had grown up struggling and fighting for everything that he possessed. And so I remained mute on the matter. As though remembering his actual mission he turned to me and said 'Go and pack your stuff, we are going.'

That declaration sounded like a final nail to my coffin and I bolted from the room. I needed to find Omolola. However new she was in my life, she mattered to me and I did not want to lose her as well. I hurried to my room throwing my clothes into my hurriedly brought out travel bag and box. I was throwing things around like a mad man until I stopped and decided to write a note for Omolola, perhaps there was a way I could get it across to her. I turned to look at Patrick who had remained quiet with the ruckus I was causing.

'We're travelling tonight' I blurted out unable to look him in the eye.

'Wow' So soon' he said; sighing in resignation and I felt a sudden sadness at my abandonment. But I was powerless with the situation.

I did not know what to say and I turned my face away as I continued to pack my things.

Chapter 2

Patrick could only watch with dismay and disappointment as Tokunbo threw clothes after clothes into his box. The boy was going away just like that, abandoning him just like everyone else in his life had. In a way he was glad but filled with mixed feelings. He would make do with his new lease of life without walking in his shadow and the handed out, hand over from the affluent Tokunbo Taylor. The boy seemed to have it all, money, looks and luck he thought with a feeling of disdain. To Patrick it seemed that Tokunbo always seemed to overcompensate by acting modest, he could not help but feel that this only increased his feelings of inadequacy. A few short hours ago he had seen him disappear with one of the prettiest girl on campus. He had had his eye on that girl and had even chatted her up but she had given him a hard rebuff and Tokunbo like prince charming with balls of steel that he seemed to have, had swept her off her feet and disappeared with her for four whole hours. Well at least he was going away and no longer with the power to cramp his game. He would miss feeding off him as he had become so used to him he thought with a feeling of loss. But then he mentally shrugged it off. He would have to survive in one way or the other without Tokunbo Taylor.

'But won't this boy even recognize and acknowledge the gravity of this sudden move? He thought with resentment lodged somewhere within him. Yes he had been in the know about his acceptance to Imperial College London, but like other things Tokunbo often kept secrets from him like the actual date of departure which was kept away from him and this sudden yanking away left him feeling as though he had been betrayed.

'Come on man' don't be like this' Tokunbo had said finally.

'I didn't say anything' Patrick replied in a steely voice.

'I know it's so soon but you know how my father is' he tried to explain still throwing things about.

As he reached for the CD player in the room, Patrick stopped him.

'You're taking that?' He asked incredulously.

had set and raised the bar for any woman for me and I had not found anyone worthy to be placed on such a pedestal. However, some had come close but I still had not experienced the magic that I had felt with her.

Ever since my reentry to his life, Patrick and I have strengthened our friendship somehow. We had corresponded through letters and met up during the very few holidays I had had when I travelled home to Lagos. But the last few years had been different; initially we seemed to have drifted apart, and I guess it had to do with my relocating to the United States of America to take up a position on Wall Street stock trade, after graduating from Imperial College London.

But with the latest summon from my father, I began to feel less in control again. I had thought that I had achieved the status of an independent, confident young man with prospects after all I did graduate tops from the University and landed a lucrative job on Wall Street! But even that was not good enough for him and I could not say anything because as much as I hated being pushed around by my father, he too had moved up the ladder and was currently the Nigerian Ambassador to Netherland.

Ever since my departure in 1990, there had been series of unrest, riots, failed elections, failed coups, imprisonment and execution of activists and general instability in the country but with this new dispensation, my father thinks that it is the right time for me to come back home and be a partaker of change and a new Nigeria. I am, however trying to share in his optimism. While I was away, I only heard the horrible news relating to my country and it was mostly heartbreaking. He called me a returnee from diaspora. It was his attempt at humor. Naturally, there seemed to be a lot of lobbying and clamor for power and governance by the emerging and old politicians. I wanted no part of it; and if my father were to insist I resolved there and then to challenge him.

Upon my arrival, I found out that not much had changed. The Political atmosphere, however was a charged one. Somehow we had managed to survive two grueling Military Juntas since my departure and the optimism for a handover to democratically elected governance seemed like a pipe dream to me. The heavy military presence at the airport did nothing to allay my fears for the country. My return, was however, one with mixed feelings. I had arrived at the immigration as a British citizen and it seemed that getting in as a foreigner was a lot easier than being a Nigerian from the courteous way in which I was treated. I risked a look at the tired and anxious faces of other travelers with Nigerian passports. Their frustration was evidently compounded by the heat and smell of that little immigration hall.

Not much had not changed. I asked Mr. John the driver to take me to the bar beach before heading towards our home in Ikoyi. Mr. John had remained in the service of my father all these years, loyally waiting on him, keeping secret all his affairs.

I sensed instant reluctance. I was surprised.

"Ah! Mr. John why now" I asked.

"What do you want to see there that you haven't seen or will not see later? He said "Nothing has changed my boy and I doubt if nothing ever will. The whole place is an eyesore." he concluded.

I winced at the reference at being called a boy, but I said nothing.

"Perhaps you would like some tea?" I offered.

"Keep your tea, it is almost midday" he answered raising and lowering his hand at the same time. I have come to discuss something with you". He was dressed in his usual native traditional attire of white lace buba and shokoto a look that he had taken up after he had been conferred with a chieftaincy title.

"You know that my 65th birthday is coming up soon, right?" he began.

"Yes daddy" I nodded in response. This was no surprise to me as mother and I had discussed it several times ever since my relocation.

'I want to throw a very private ball, black tie and all.' He announced.

'Ok' I said as if I knew what it entailed to throw a ball in our society, but knowing my father, it was best to agree with him even if you didn't know what he was talking about.

"You know Yewande, your cousin is now an event planner and the last work she did at the President's banquet hall in Aso Rock was a very grand affair so she will be handling this one and I will be having a few politicians and people from the consulate in attendance. So, it must be a grand affair with minimal press coverage. 'And one more thing,' he said pausing for effect. 'I am also having Chief Binuyo and his family in attendance"

'Ok' I thought, giving myself a mental shrug, while I tried to remember who Chief Binuyo was, but I suddenly began to wonder why he was telling me. As though reading my mind, he continued.

"I want you to meet his daughter Foluke, she is a very beautiful girl and I want you two to get to know each other".

I felt a rise of irritation within me and I barely managed to conceal my anger. I was tired of meeting these Lagos girls from the so called rich homes in Ikoyi whose egos required constant stroking.

"Look son" he continued ignoring the anger on my face.

'There is no harm in meeting her, if you like her then ask her out, if you don't, no harm, no foul.' He said with both hands raised in the air. But remember I am retired with this birthday o".

"But daddy I ought to be able to choose the girl I would like to date by myself?" I asked him

"I am not saying that you cannot choose a girl for yourself but you will have to meet her through someone somewhere won't you? I just think that this girl would be suitable for you". He said.

"Or for you" I thought quietly knowing that my father always had his own agenda and business interest in everything he did. As much as he tried to conceal his affairs with his various mistresses, I always knew a thing or two about it.

"Anyway just think about it". He concluded.

He soon began to regale me with stories of how he had met my mother. A story I had heard thousands of time. He often enjoyed reminiscing about his younger days of how he won the affections of my mother with his grass to grace stories. Then, before I could chip in he asked me to get a sheet of paper and began to reel off names of guests that he thinks scanning the dimly lit hall as though looking for her companion. An usher walked up to her to help and she momentarily had her back to me. She had on a dress that shimmered in the dark, her green emerald dress was backless and this gave me a clear advantage of her creamy smooth skin. I continued to gawk at her until Patrick whistled and nudged me.

'Who is that? He whispered.

'I don't know but I'm about to find out' I replied and got to my feet

Like a moth to a flame, I walked up to her and said 'Hello! Perhaps I can help you'

As soon as she looked up at me I was even more enthralled by her beauty. She was simply stunning. I had developed a bit of the American accent and often times I had to speak a bit more Nigerian if I was to be understood at work but whenever I felt the need to be impressive I would switch up the ante a bit and this evening was no exception. I had sounded so foreign that it almost felt alien to speak without a foreign accent.

"Hello' she responded almost flirtatiously.

'Am not sure where I'm supposed to seat but I am here with my parents Chief Binuyo' she smiled as she said this.

'Okay she isn't so bad' I thought, as a recollection of the conversation I had had with my father came rushing to my mind. I introduced myself and she did the same. So this was Foluke, I had been preparing myself for someone else but not this gorgeous girl. Maybe my father was right after all. I steered her towards her parents table. As we walked on, I gently placed my hand on the curve of her back and my hand came in contact with the softest and smoothest of skin. She was warm and I was sorry when I had to take my hand away.

Due to the many demands on me that night I managed to extract her away for a moment and I quickly collected her phone number. I had begged Patrick to keep an eye on her for me while I went to take family photos with the celebrant. Patrick found a way to tease me about her as he made whipping sounds every time I walked past his table to attend to one guest or the other. Patrick helped by talking to her while I attended to my parent's guests. But I was in a daze all night long and I longed for her companionship. That night I forgot about my quest to find Omolola Bailey as I eventually spent the rest of the night talking and dancing with Foluke. Later on, I must have seemed like a most ungracious host to my friends as I stuck to Foluke's side like a leech that night totally besotted. Foluke was a sweet and lively woman who soon had me infatuated. I wanted to know all there was to know about her and so much more.

Our first date had been at the prestigious Ocean View restaurant on the island. I was even more impressed by the fact that she opted for us to seat outdoor as against the indoor restaurant. It was a warm and beautiful night and the gentle breeze from the sea seemed to add a bit of magic to a promising night ahead. Dinner was part of a three course meal. She declined taking any alcohol with any of her meals and this led to a lengthen discussion about alcohol. She told me that she was 'born again' but I didn't think that she said this in order to put me off from having carnal intentions towards her because she was very hip and current about the things of the world. We were able to laugh about so many things that night as I got to know her even more. She didn't strike me as the fanatical religious type. She told me about her mentor Pastor Deroju and that she was a member of one of the funky but liberal new generation churches which allowed her to dress however she wanted to their church services and was not as stiff as the Orthodox Church her parents attended.

She was already working for her father's Estate Management Company on the Island having just completed her youth service to the nation. However when she told me that she had initially attended a Polytechnic and later on the University of Abuja, I had been a little surprised because I was initially prejudiced against students who went to the Polytechnic back when I was a student in Unilag but all that changed when I was in the University at Imperial College. My prospective began to change after I interacted with people from all over the world. But it still took me as a surprise when I heard this. She had such impeccable manners and was well informed about current affairs. Her taste in music and lifestyle made me see her as someone that would match my lifestyle.

Her sense of humor matched mine and we had a lot in common that by the end of the date I knew I wanted her. However, I did not want her to think that I was rushing her when I asked to see her the next day for lunch. But when she agreed to the lunch date, I wasted no time in asking her to be my girlfriend.

Perhaps I ought to have been cautious after our first sexual encounter which had taken place almost immediately after our second date but I was blinded by my lust for her that I agreed to the seemingly impossible terms that she set out for me.

No doubt the chemistry was a good one and my attraction to Foluke had been equally strong that it was almost physically impossible to stop my body from responding to her the way it did after our first kiss in the car when I had gone to drop her off after our long lunch date. Her response was very encouraging and I knew that our body chemistry was in sync with each other. There was no need for pretence when she came to my flat that weekend as I lured her to my bed that day and for a while she replaced Omolola who was the chief object of my masturbatory fantasies. We spent that weekend getting to know each other even more intimately than I could envision. I was convinced that this was the woman for me, because she not only complimented my physical needs, we were psychologically in tune too. But the next time I wanted to initiate another sexual encounter, I was met with rebuff and a stiff resistance. This puzzled me because Foluke had not come across to me as the type of girl to play games nor was she unsure of herself. She began to give the excuse that she had felt that it was too early in the relationship to be involved sexually especially after barely knowing each other for two weeks and that as a born again Christian it was against her beliefs and would harm her spirituality.

It was a little off putting for me and I was mildly irritated by her sudden break off of the spell that had bonded me to her. She came off as being sophisticated and adventurous to me in the past two weeks that I had come to know her but all of a sudden there was this new cautious and timid girl who was launching a preemptive strike on sabotaging our growing relationship with her beliefs.

'Tokunbo, Toks', she said in between kisses.

'I think we should stop doing this' she said gently and firmly pushing me away from her. We had been lying on my couch, making out and I was thinking of taking her either there or in my bed room.

'I don't understand why we should stop making love' I told her as soon as she dropped the bombshell to me.

'We are moving too fast and I would prefer to get to know you more, but not like this' she said as she took her hands away from mine. I had been sucking on her fingers when she did this and it made me realize the seriousness in her voice.

I tried to make light of it by responding. 'How else can we know each other than making hot love?' I asked drawing her to me once more? But she got up and put a distance between us by walking barefooted towards the door, even though her shoes were still by the floor beside my feet I noticed the defiant look on her face and I asked her.

'You're serious aren't you?'

She gave a firm nod.

'Come on, this is childish!' my irritation fueled by my hard-on which I could not be bothered to hide.

In my lust filled mind I could not understand why she was putting up a wall between us. I gradually began to change my mind about her. If she was not going to put out anymore due to her beliefs, I had to respect her but find company elsewhere. I did not want to come off as a monster or some sort of sexual deviant. But I still wanted her because sex with her was rather nice and satisfying. But with these new laid down conditions? I was not sure how to move on with a sexless relationship. But I figured that it was too early to be having issues with the relationship and so I agreed with her.

Just then my phone rang and it was Patrick who informed me that he was on his way to my apartment. Hearing this, Foluke decided to make her escape and insisted on leaving before Patrick's arrival I did not understand this sudden change in plans but I assumed that she was shy of letting Patrick know that she was already visiting with me so soon.

Barely five minutes after her departure Patrick arrived and we got talking. He invited me to an exclusive party scheduled later that night and with that I gradually pushed the thought of Foluke out of my mind, determined to catch my fun that night.

She kept her distance and a week later Patrick and I were invited to another birthday party where one of the big boys in town was using the party to show off his latest acquisition of the latest 5 series BMW. I was curious about the new car and I was thinking of getting either the Mercedes G Wagon or a BMW too, so going to the party would afford me an opportunity to closely inspect the car. As soon as we got to the marquee tent that was the venue of the party that night we were immediately overwhelmed by the music the DJ was churning out through heavy box like speakers. The dance floor was already filled with couple dancing to the fast rising international Nigerian musicians like Paul Play Dairo whose remix of his father's legendary track was a hit in the country and a testament to the type of music from Nigeria which was threatening to take over the continent and the world for that matter. Patrick seemed to know almost everyone there and I began to worry that I would be an outsider there until I spotted a group of mutual friends and a cousin or two of mine. Eventually I got into the feel of the party and was drinking champagne like an alcoholic when a feeling of de javu began to wash over me.

The Deejay had switched to some hip hop music that had been in vogue while we were at the university when I caught sight of her. Even though I had seen her only once and spent an amazing few hours of one single night a decade ago, I could not forget those lovely hazel eyes of that beautiful girl who captured and enthralled me many years ago.

It was as though my eyes knew that some other pair of eyes had been fixated on mine in that crowded room, when I glanced up across the room to see her staring at me in a way that sent an unfamiliar shiver down the back of my neck. I must have given off a look of surprise because I saw a corner of her lips lift up in a slow smile. She was stunning and had even grown more beautiful than I remembered. She had on a black tee shirt which she paired off with a dark blue pair of jeans and her long hair was packed in a tight pony tail, leaving her beautiful face exposed. A reminder of how she looked the first night that we met many years ago. As though on cue, we both began to move towards each other and when she stopped in her tracks, I turned to follow the direction of her eyes and noticed that they flickered towards Patrick who was watching her too. But I continued in my stride towards her obliterating everything and everyone just to get to her. Her stare had returned to me and this time she was smiling openly with recognition written all over her face.

'Tokunbo Taylor! She announced as I got to her.

Omolola I blurted out in answer.

I had always played out the different scenarios' in my head of what I would say and how I would play it cool per chance that I ran into her again. Seeing her however threw me off balance and I was standing dumb struck and tongue tied in her presence. Silently she nodded and struck out her hand in an offer of handshake.

I wanted to enclose her in a huge hug to feel her fully formed figure against me and not let go. Instead, I took her outstretched hand and shook it more vigorously than I had intended. Even her grip was electrifying as it sent all manner of heat waves coursing through my body. I continued to hold on to her hand, not wanting to let go lest she disappear again from my life. But then a guy walked up to us and handed her a cocktail glass. The way he draped his arm over her shoulder made me to drop her hand as quickly as I could. For a moment I was filled with conflicting emotions as I could not bear the look of that arm across her shoulders.

'Oh hi' she turned to him and then proceeded to introduce us.

'This is Tokunbo Taylor an old friend of mine, way back from Unilag' she declared and continued. 'Tokunbo abandoned us for greener pastures abroad and is back now'. She said giving off more information that was in my opinion necessary to this arrogant and cocky looking fellow.

'This is Akin my boyfriend' she announced twisting the knife a little deeper.

Because he was holding a drink in his other hand, he had to lift this offending arm off her and offer it to me. I looked at the out stretched hand and took it in a firm grip to test his strength. I must admit that he matched me strength for strength. Nevertheless, I was excited to see her and we began to converse as though Akin was not present.

'Wow it has been a decade' I said trying to make light of how I was really feeling.

'Yes it has. I am surprised that you remember me' she replied nodding rapidly.

I knew what I wanted to say to her and the other many things I wanted to say to her but I couldn't, not with Akin and the loud music blaring from the speakers close by and in such an environment. So what was she doing with this guy I wondered, she could do better I thought as I sized him up.

'I saw you in the City People soft sell magazine, Mr. Eligible bachelor' she yelled tapping me gently on the chest.

I gave a laugh in response as I continued to size her companion up. I was at least a foot taller than him and wondered what he did for a living.

Because the music was loud, I did not hear what Akin said next, but I was relieved when he excused himself away from us.

It was as though history was repeating itself and I asked her to follow me outside the tent so that I could talk to her. As we walked out, I saw Patrick give me a funny look which I ignored. I was not going to let this opportunity pass me by.

As soon as we got outside, I seized her into a bear hug and instantly felt her response to me. It was strange that after all these years this wonderful girl still had an effect over me that left me feeling so excited and refreshingly different.

She broke off the hug as abruptly as it began and stepped away from me. I looked into her face and she spoke up for me.

'You owe me an explanation' she said as if the years had not passed us by.

I was taken aback because she remembered.

'I am sorry' I blurted out. This was not the way I had imagined that the conversation would be, when and if we were ever to have one.

Before I could say anything more she burst out laughing upon seeing my contrite expression and said

'Hey I am just messing with you' and switched the conversation to ask me where I worked and what I was up to. I told her with words that I could not get fast enough out of my mouth whilst wanting only to know all I could about her instead.

As we began to converse, there were so many things that I wanted to say to her but the environment just did not seem right and it bothered me that she had a boyfriend who was probably lurking somewhere. I was not afraid of him. It was the idea that she had a boyfriend that bothered me so much.

I managed to make enough small talk with her that night and I got all her contacts and details.

She was working for a small law firm in Ikeja and was planning to go for her masters in Petroleum law. I was impressed with her academic tenacity and pursuit and I told her so.

She shrugged it off as though it was not a big deal and we

exchanged numbers. The phone number she had given me was her neighbor's and I told her that I would call her and I did just that the next morning, leaving a message with the person who picked and informed me that she had gone for church service, I informed the receiver that I would call back in the afternoon.

I was in such a state that I counted the minutes and the hours and checked my phone every chance I got while I waited.

As soon as she took my call, I made it a date to see to see her that same day. If it meant me travelling out of the Island to the Mainland I would do just that but she insisted on meeting me half way and we agreed to meet somewhere in Surulere the central part of the city. While I waited for her in my Mitsubishi SUV at the car park of the restaurant that she had chosen, I wondered about her and there was no doubt about my intentions for her. I hoped to date her and make her mine. I was excited by the second opportunity of having her back in my life. It felt as though my search for the perfect woman had just come to an end and I looked forward to it.

As soon as she alighted from the yellow taxi that brought her, I took a moment to watch her. She exuded confidence and poise that many girls I dated did not have and for a moment the thought of Foluke crossed my mind and I felt a slight twinge of guilt. Because I could not waste any more precious moment, I shoved the thought to the back of my mind and approached her. We were soon seated in the restaurant and I just could not stop looking at her. I ordered for some drinks and as she sat across the table from me I remembered that she even looked more beautiful than I could remember as emotion laced with memories of that night swirled in my head. Her caramel complexion was her best features and I longed to touch her intimately. But first I needed all the answers to my questions about her and I wasted no time asking her about herself and everything I needed to know. She was squatting with her friend Abimbola in Ojota, a suburb on the mainland and complained about commuting to work as a nightmare with the traffic situation in the city of Lagos. She had been staying with her friend for about a year now but regularly visited her parents in the family house in Egbeda, a place that seemed like another planet to me. She explained to me how she was looking forward to studying for her master's programme and would love to travel out of the country for it but as it was she was working hard to pay her rent and her bills. From the off handed way she spoke about her boyfriend Akin I could tell that it was not a serious relationship and knowing that an opportunity like this might not come again I decided to reveal my own agenda as I teasingly told her that she could do better than the Akin fellow.

'What makes you so sure?' she asked as she took a sip of the orange drink that she had agreed to take.

'You are way out of his league' I answered.

'And whose league do I belong to?' She teased me back. I was encouraged by her open and wanton flirt and I drove right in.

'Let me take care of you' I said watching her expression change from that of coyness to one of surprise.

'Wow!' She exclaimed 'You are so direct.'

'I don't believe in wasting any time since I know what I want and I am not about to let go a second time' I said seriously. A series of emotions crossed her face and it was impossible for me to know what she was thinking as I waited for her response.

'You're asking me out?' She said finally. 'Don't you already have a girlfriend and don't lie to me because I will find out' she warned me.

Just then the thought of Foluke and my father crossed my mind and I decided to be truthful with her.

'Well there is someone' I hesitated

'But like you it's not so serious.' I prevaricated when it seemed as though she were having an Ah-Ha moment. 'I think I have been holding out for you because I still remember us from Unilag' I confessed barring for the first time my innermost feelings to this wonderful girl who could make or break my heart.

It was her turn to be shy now as she could not meet my searching eyes. I wished I could know what she was thinking. Her expression was inscrutable.

When she finally spoke she said 'You were the first boy that ever broke my heart and even though we had just one amazing night a decade ago which by the way I am surprised that you still remember. It took a really long time for me to get over you and now that you are back barely twenty four hours after seeing me again, you want me to pick up from where you left me ten years ago'.

I gave a sad sigh as I told her that she was not being fair to me that the circumstances for my leaving then was beyond my power and I was young but I was now asking for another chance for us to rekindle that flame which I added silently to myself never quite burned out.

'But not even a word from you?' She demanded and I knew that I could make all the excuses especially how Patrick had looked for her on my behalf and did not find her because he did not meet her that day so long ago.

'Omolola,' I said holding the hand that she had placed on the table before us. 'We can rehash what went wrong or how long we have been apart. I want you to give me another chance say yes and you won't ever regret it' I declared. Before she could respond I reached over and planted a kiss on her lips, not caring that we were in a public restaurant. Her response was instantaneous as it was warm and well received as soon as we broke apart I could sense that we were in one accord.

What began as a simple date became a full blown relationship as I committed every spare time I had to Omolola. I even ignored and abandoned Foluke and Patrick as I came up with every excuse to be with Omolola. I could not seem to get enough of her. Having wanted her for so long I knew that I had to work with her pace and I was glad that I did not have to wait too long to possess her; body and soul. She, on her part broke up with her boyfriend Akin whom she confessed that she was not so serious about. We began to make plans together and I really wanted to build a life with this amazing woman who continued to intrigue me every day as I got to know her even more. For the first time I felt I was truly happy and content with a woman. She fulfilled all my fantasies and I was totally and head over heels in love with her. Omolola unleashed in me skills and thrills that I had never experienced with any other woman and I devoured all she had to offer. She told me all I needed to know about her. She was the first born out of five siblings, her civil servants parents were on the verge of retirement from the government parastatals that they both worked at. She was not born with a silver spoon like I was and she valued hard work and diligence above anything. She told me about the many battles with lecturers and men that she constantly fought off to be taken seriously on account of her looks and her resilience at resisting temptations to get ahead. My admiration for her grew even more. Here was a woman who clearly knew what she wanted and was willing to work for it.

I was hoping for a total lockdown on this relationship by making love to Omolola, praying that she did not have any hang up like Foluke had. It was a sunny Saturday when I picked her from the bus park at CMS and she happily hopped into my car. She had insisted on taking the bus to meet me on the Island instead of having me drive all the way to her apartment and back to the Island just to hang out. I was even more stoked by her consideration and vowed that I would take better care of her.

I knew now that this was the woman for me and we were going to be together forever.

Chapter 4

2018

As soon as Omolola got into her luxurious chauffeur driven SUV a sense of foreboding began to wash over as she struggled to control her emotions. She was going down a memory lane that she did not want to revisit. She had remembered the last time that she saw him; the memory of that moment always had her tingling with remembrance. He had come straight to her place after work that Friday night from the island to the tiny apartment that she shared with friend and roommate Abimbola on the mainland. As soon as he saw that she was alone he had hurriedly gathered her to himself as if he had not seen her in ages and swept her up as though she weighed nothing. It had also been their last intimate encounter together and it had been different, desperate even and her body had known before her heart what was about to happen and what had happened. But the difference had not been with her body alone, Tokunbo had been different too his voracious and passionate desire for her had been so fierce, it was almost feudalistic. It felt as though he was giving her all that he could. He had clung to Omolola as though he was being deprived of his life and if his soul were to be a physical thing she could almost touch it. So much that he tried to speak but could not coherently voice out his feelings and he said words that were almost meaningless. The flames which consumed them both that night always left her shivering with raw remembered emotions just as she was now.

Her driver noticed her shivering and politely asked if he should reduce the temperature if it was too cold but she dismissed him curtly as she returned to her thoughts. Even now the years of torture of not being able to reclaim or lay stake to that passion, had only ignited her ambition to become a successful and accomplished lawyer. When her firm had been asked to represent the Belema community, in

Rivers state concerning OSCRON's encroachment and pollution of their ecological atmosphere she had put aside every other case as she prepared brief on the matter. Knowing that she would probably see Tokunbo Taylor again she had to look the part of the no nonsense hard-hitting and successful lawyer she had become. After her experience with Tokunbo, she had become an over-thinker who over the years had learnt that it was best to keep busy than to limit her time analyzing and wondering about how her life would have been had they stayed together.

She went further back in time to the year 2000 by remembering how her heart had almost lurched out of her chest as soon as she saw him because she knew who he was. She silently wondered if he would remember her. He was even better looking than her memories of him, and she remembered every detail of him even after ten years of dreaming about the first boy she had ever given her heart to on a beautiful night, during a walk along the moonlight Lagos lagoon.

Under hooded eyes she had followed his every movement and was more aware of him than any other person in that crowded Marquee. Ever since that fateful night almost a decade ago when in her girlish fantasy she had dreamed that he at least felt something or anything for her or even remembered their amazing night together, she always dreamt that he would return to her. She had never forgotten that first night when she had bared her soul to him and he had disappeared like a puff of smoke. She had felt a sense of loss as she was teased and tortured by his abandonment. Even though they had not been physical she felt that they had connected otherwise. Over the years the longing for him had only grown as she looked for him in any guy that she dated or any who approached her for a relationship.

Sometimes she blamed herself for putting him on a pedestal; Tokunbo Taylor had been a yardstick of measure to any man that she knew. He was as handsome and tall just the way her fantasy man ought to be. She had held onto the dream that one day their paths would cross in a way that she could only imagine.

The music under the marquee had been as loud as it could be and she felt her ear drums threatening to burst. She had read about him in the City's soft sell magazine which had had the news of his father's extravagant birthday party that had the cream of the society in attendance. There was also a reference to Tokunbo as being one of the top 50 eligible bachelors in Lagos City. The picture in the magazine had not been able to capture him the way she imagined it should. So here he was looking like something from a cosmopolitan magazine exuding style and poise the way a handsome man who was aware of his looks and its effect on women should. 'I am probably a forgotten or struck out number on his shelf— life list of acquired women' she thought miserably. Perhaps if he did remember her she would be an accomplished notch to his bed post. She mused as her eyes followed his every movement. People were constantly shaking and hugging him and the way he held on to his drink made her suddenly hot as she imagined his hands on her body.

She must have willed him to look at her because as soon as he saw her a tremendous amount of relief washed over as she saw the way his eyes lit up in recognition. As if on cue they both began to move towards each other and like a fairy tale her fantasies came true. As they got reacquainted she saw the truth and the eagerness in his eyes and she knew that they were destined to be together. She could hardly wait as her excitement to be reacquainted was evident in her every action. But she knew that he had to take the first step.

Her neighbour's message had her smiling when she learnt that a certain Tokunbo Taylor had called twice and would be calling again at 3:30 p.m. for her. She quickly rushed to her neighbor's place to wait for his call on their landline. He owed her an explanation and besides she still had his wrist watch from that fateful night as a memento.

Meeting with him soon revealed a passion that she had had for him come to surface and she was encouraged by his eagerness to begin a relationship which left her wanting more and more of him.

But now she continued to remember how he had in the aftermath of their afterglow, gone on holding her tightly, closely and reverently looking into her eyes as though he could bury himself in them. Being in his arms that night felt like she was wrapped in his warmth and love as she had laid her head upon his chest listening to the tumultuous pounding of his heart and she felt hers beat against his body. His gentle stroking of her breasts began a gradual arousal as it reignited their already spent passion and their mouths soon found each other again. It was that moment that she had often though about in her private and quiet moments. Later it baffled her at how gullible she had been to believe that that moment had been real for him. He was a Lagos Yoruba demon. And now more than a decade later, after a close encounter with him at the meeting, he had tried to talk to her and she had refused him an audience. She had to make him believe that she was impervious to him. She would not betray her heavily guarded heart twice over for Tokunbo

Taylor. The pain never quite went away.

From what she could remember their parting had been painful. After such an intense and passionate love making Tokunbo had left her to sleep and she remembered how she had looked forward to his phone call the next morning on the satellite mobile phone that he had given her. It was a very rare commodity back in the early 2000s to have a mobile phone in Lagos. Back then it was a common sight to see long queues at phone booths, with everyone waiting for his or her turn to make calls. This was before the advent of GSM phones. She had to carry that huge device in her hand bag that morning and she smiled as she remembered how she considered herself one of the privileged few to own such a device. She didn't feel as though she was reaching for some height, after all she was a legal practitioner now having been called to bar a few years ago against all odds.

But the call she got that morning was not the one that she was expecting. Tokunbo's father Ambassador Oriyomi Taylor had called her summoning her to his mansion in Ikoyi for a chat. With trepidation, she had asked Abimbola to accompany her to the residence in Ikoyi and her roommate had happily obliged. As Abimbola drove in her Volkswagen beetle car, on that sunny Saturday morning Omolola had sat back wondering and fretting, replaying the conversation on the phone over and over in her head. The man had been curt and went straight to the point; he had introduced himself in a voice which she knew was used to being obeyed. The constant chatter of her companion had eased the same sense of foreboding she felt now as they approached the residence. She had never entered the mansion as Tokunbo had only pointed it out to her once when he had taken her for a drive along the suburbs of Ikoyi. She had marveled at the huge residence from a distance and from what she could see behind the huge fence and security presence. As soon as they arrived at the massive gatehouse they were allowed access in and Abimbola had whistled under her breath at the sheer opulence of the compound. There was a short drive way to a huge mansion which she suspected was the main house as she counted three buildings situated on an expanse of an acre of land. There was an impressive array of garage doors which displayed a small fleet of expensive and exotic cars. She had felt even smaller in the Volkswagen.

A steward had led them into the building through huge Italic columns and what she saw took her breath away when they entered the foyer where a huge display of an assorted arrangement of fresh flowers had overwhelmed their senses. Abimbola had looked as clearly intimidated as she did and both of them sat on the edges of their seat at the guest waiting lounge, a room which looked like something out of a luxurious home design magazine. The gold damask wall paper covering was an exact match to the lounge chairs in which they sat in and she longed to trace her fingers along the exquisite gold carving etched on the white polished wood of the chair. The huge French windows were softly concealed by long white curtains that seemed to float from the ceiling and everywhere reflected beauty and splendor.

Cold drinks were instantly provided without being asked but Omolola was too nervous to drink anything. She was still not sure why she had been summoned as they waited in silence which was occasionally broken by Abimbola asking questions that she had no answers to. Chief Oriyomi definitely knew how to keep one waiting she thought as she looked at her wrist watch for the umpteenth time. She was still wearing the same watch that Tokunbo had given her many years ago. The suspense was making the knots in her stomach tighten the more and Omolola braced herself for the meeting ahead. After what seemed like an hour a smartly dressed steward came to inform her that the Ambassador was ready to see her. She gave Abimbola a nervous glance before making her way after the man.

If the waiting room had been impressive, the massive living room was spectacular as she was led into the grand room. Chief Oriyomi Taylor was every bit of how she imagined him to be, tall and handsome like Tokunbo. Although Tokunbo was taller in comparison to his father, she could see the same mannerisms and gestures in him. Chief Oriyomi was looking at her with such an odd expression that set off some alarm in her. The man had clearly not expected this paragon of beauty before him and he could understand why his son was smitten by this wonder of exquisite beauty. For a moment or two he was sorry about what he was about to do but his plans and ambitions were far too important to be truncated by such a distraction.

Omolola had genuflected as a sign of respect to him in greeting when she saw him and he responded warmly to her. She looked around her in awe and wonder and had to mentally kick herself to order. She suspected that he would try to put her at ease as he could sense her discomfiture. He begun by asking her, what her surname was, and what she did for a living. She was sure that he was only asking her these questions when he probably had the answers from Tokunbo. He had a grandiosity she could not help but be overwhelmed by. He asked what her parents did and who they were almost as if he were trying to weigh her net worth through his inquiries. He told her that he was asking her those questions because he needed to know if he knew anyone of note that was related to her, when he said this Omolola was not initially sure that she heard him right because of the way her heart was pounding in her ears but she shrugged off the feeling it left her and tried to concentrate on him whilst she concluded that he did not really care about any of what she was saying. There was something rather condescending about him.

The truth was that he was trying to disarm her. However he could not fail to show the distaste in his face when he learnt that her parents were low end civil servants. On Chief Oriyomi's part he could sense that there was something about this girl that was clearly disarming. There was an essence of naivety about her as well as strength of character. Qualities he wished that Tokunbo had. As she talked, he began to admire her confidence and her poise. It was almost intimidating and he smiled at her. He wondered just how serious her relationship with Tokunbo was; in any case he didn't care as long as it did not derail his meticulously laid plans. He began to talk about himself a habit that she was sure he loved immensely as he boasted about his achievements and material possessions. He knew that he had to implement his social dominance and he mentally calculated how to make her feel inferior based on his assumption of her family's net worth. At some point Omolola found it increasingly hard to keep a straight and polite face as she waited for his implied insinuation?

Before she could help herself she blurted out 'Why have you asked me to come?

For a moment or two, Chief Oriyomi was taken aback and corked his head to one side while he took a long look at her.

In response he got up and walked towards a door which she had not noticed existed as it was cleverly concealed in the same wall paper motif that adorned the room. When he came back, he was holding a huge brown envelope and Omolola suddenly had a bad premonition. When he saw the look on her face, he smiled again, with the smile that he often used to disarm his opponents when going in for the kill. He noticed that her composure had changed and this pleased him in some way. As he took his time to lower himself into the settee he had previously occupied, her eyes followed his every unhurried movements while she waited for his response to her question.

How long have you been seeing Tokunbo? He asked her instead.

'Almost two months now' she said but added quickly 'but I have known him for ten years now.' Omolola and Tokunbo had spent a considerable amount of time together and had grown so close that she had been hoping to confide in her mother about him. The woman had been looking forward to her meeting someone of note but this meeting with his father was not how she had imagined it would be orchestrated.

'Really!' He said raising an eyebrow "funny he never mentioned you once" he announced.

But before she could go further he cleared his throat and said.

'You asked me why I asked you to come, this tells me that you are a very smart girl and I will tell you why. Tokunbo tells me that you would want to do your master's degree programme in Law in the United Kingdom.' He declared.

Omolola was not sure if he was telling her or asking her and so she nodded as a glimmer of hope began coursing through her. Perhaps the man was going to recommend an institution for her and probably influence her education she thought; after all he was a very influential man.

'I will be your sponsor, all expenses paid in full' he said as he noticed the effect his declaration was having on her. Before she could say anything he added 'Provided you leave my son alone!'

It was like watching a theatrical piece as her face switched with a conflict of emotions ranging from hope to shock and to bewilderment.

His words sank into her like a rock being thrown into the bottom of river as her thoughts rushed around her mind in torrents. She tried to heave a sad sigh but her breath got caught in her throat. It was as though he had physically slapped her in the face and she reeled from its imaginary impact.

'You know, he cannot be serious about you if it is has only been what, two months? I would not want you wasting your life over my son's indiscretion.'

"Indiscretion?" She blurted out as that was the only word that she could think of.

'Tokunbo is set to marry my good friend Chief Binuyo's daughter Foluke and as we speak Foluke is in Geneva buying her bridal trousseau and baby things.'

It was as though her heart wanted to stop beating and she froze as Chief Oriyomi dropped one bombshell after another. Omolola became numb as she sat shell shocked while he continued to rip her apart with his words.

'I wouldn't want there to be a scandal as I feel you should be compensated for my son's indiscretion.'

'Indiscretion' she thought to herself.

'Was there no other word to describe this fiasco?' His words had created even more of an internecine war within her. She felt that she had taken in a lifetime of information within thirty seconds.

Suddenly her numbness gave way to rage and she stood up so suddenly and quickly as though bitten by a bug.

'Thank you, but no thank you for your'.... She hesitated and when she could find the word she added 'generous offer' she said as she drew on the strap of her bag and in the process felt the weight of the satellite mobile phone in her bag. She quickly reached inside and she pulled out the device and laid it carefully on the seat that she had vacated.

'I will see myself out if you don't mind' she said in a steely voice that she did not recognize.

'Come now, he said don't be silly. You don't know what I am offering you yet. Take this' he said, waving a paper at her. Her first instinct was to grab it and rip it to shreds but she stopped and half turned to look at him. It was going to be a battle of wits as she stood there undecided. She knew that she would not take the check but some will so powerful beyond her comprehension would not allow her legs to move.

Chief Oriyomi smiled as he felt that he had finally got to her at last.

Chapter 5

Meeting room 234 was the venue of my next meeting and I was running late. As I hurried towards it, I had a feeling of de javu about me. But then, there was nothing unusual about going into room 234 for a meeting. I could not count the number of times I had used the room to attend or conduct meetings, so I wondered why I was feeling at odds with myself as I approached the room.

It has been 18 years since I last felt such an excitement about a woman the way I did with Omolola. Seeing her again today brought back that same rush and knotting in my stomach. I wonder how God could allow just one person to have such a tremendous effect on me. I had been invited by the HR to attend the meeting with some lawyers representing the Belema community in Rivers state where we had some conflicts in business interests; they were suing our company on the infringement to their fundamental human rights. Naturally, as the Head of finance I was to be present at this meeting. As soon as she walked into the meeting with her colleagues I knew who she was. She was even more beautiful and had kept her figure. Although the name had changed it was now Omolola Williams. If she recognized me, she gave no indication as introductions were made all round the conference table in our exclusive meeting room where we often held such delicate and high powered meetings.

I could not seem to keep my eyes off her as she displayed poise, competence and skill which showed how good she was at her job. As she stated their case in a voice that was ever so soft yet with a steely persuasion, I watched and marveled at her tenacity and aptitude. Her acquisitiveness for her client's case was clearly permeated in her defense and I was impressed by her eloquence and experience and if it were down to my decision alone, I would have given her whatever they asked for. However I had a job to do and so the meeting progressed with my mind wandering on and off. I remembered her vividly especially in the throes of passion when she would shut her eyes tightly as she neared her peak. I could feel myself hardening by the very thought of this and I drew a hand across my face feeling the hot breath against the skin of my hand all the while remembering it as though it were yesterday how her hotness burned against the skin of my neck. This was a woman whom I had shown with my body what I was experiencing with my soul and now I know that she was going to be the death of me. As I continued to watch her I could not help but notice how her impeccably groomed ring less free fingers were as it held on to her pen with which she gesticulated with as she made her point. Her suit was a designer's cut which gave a testimony of its own that she was comfortable if not wealthy and it accentuated her form perfectly. She had a beautiful pixie haircut and the curls on her fore head perfectly accentuated her cheek bones. As I continued to look at her, a comparison began to form in my mind as her classical chic look made my wife Foluke's dowdy and somber looks now very evident.

After an interminable discussion, we eventually came to a settlement with them and we ended the meeting. Since it was customary for the company to provide lunch or dinner for clients, depending on the time such meetings or arbitrations ended, I was hoping to get a chance to be reacquainted with her. But they declined our offer.

And as they were departing, I cornered her as though it was on an official capacity but I knew I had to see her again.

Omolola…. I began.

'Ah Mr. Taylor. It is Mrs. Williams to you.' She said in a voice that did not encourage any familiarity. Her ringing phone saved me from the awkwardness of the situation and prevented her from saying anything further and she indicated her eagerness to take the call. From that pronouncement, I could deduce that she wanted to keep things professional and I also detected a frostiness from her which put me in my place.

Why was she so foreign? What was her problem? We had both gone our respective ways due to her bailing out on me. If there was anyone who should hold a grudge it should be me but as a Christian I have learnt to forgive and forget. But then, did I really forget? This carnal flesh is so weak. Yet I could not help myself from thinking about her again as I remembered how her breathe felt against my chest when she laid on it and how I have never felt so close or so near any other woman like I did with her. I had been possessed with a hard on throughout the meeting and it was with a sheer will that I was even able to stand at all. Where was this needy feeling coming from? I saw lots of beautiful women daily at work and at meetings and none had ever had this effect on me. I am a happily married man with a grown up son, so where was this weakness coming from? But I could not shake off an uncompromising injunction that began to resonate in my head, as lustful feelings and a sort of vulnerability that I had for this woman seemed to engulf me.

'Get thee behind me!' was one of a favorite litany that I sometimes chanted in jest, to keep me from falling into temptation, it came to mind now. For many years now my life and lifestyle had changed profoundly from the carefree young man I had been in my youth. I was now an astute businessman, a loving family man and a devoted born again Christian ever since I had given my life to Christ and like a recovering addict I had a sponsor in Pastor Aremu Johnson. He was the one person that I shared everything with, my hopes and fears, my spirituality.

Shortly after the birth of my first son I left the bank where I worked and moved to OSCRON oil company and my life had been full of series of accomplishments, business wise and professionally. A few years later, Foluke and I went on to have another child who I named Niniola our beautiful but autistic daughter who after gracing us with her charms was called to God's side when she turned three. Nevertheless I am proud to say that we have continued to live comfortable and privileged lives and the added glory is our faith and conversion as born again Christians. We did have some other challenges especially when my father the family patriarch had a mild stroke some ten years ago. It had been a wakeup call for all of us as the devil tried all he could to destroy the family but to the glory of God we overcame all obstacles. I must confess that sometimes I still feel the heavy handedness of my father on me even after all these years, despite the fact that I have taken over the responsibility of giving him a befitting retirement life. He still remained relevant in business circles. Yet somehow his frustrations of unrealized ambitions for me are blamed on me.

Perhaps, I should go after her and demand some explanations. But won't that be a little too late; after all it has been almost 18 years now. As I made to move, I suddenly remembered that it was Wednesday and I had mid-week service to attend at the Christian Rapture Savers Church where I was a church leader. Sometimes, work schedule meant that I miss some of the services and meetings but I tried as much as I could to clear my schedule for it and today was not going to be an exception, old flame or not.

Later, as my driver drove me towards the Church, I marveled at how far we have come in the building of this magnificent edifice. From a tiny tent of worshippers we have grown to this height of Christendom. I am so proud of the work we do for those unbelievers out there that do not know the truth and the love of God. We try as much as possible to bring them to his fold every way we can and that is one of the things I find so alluring about Pastor Aremu Johnson a self-taught theologian whose heavenly call had been so divine. He always knows the needs and the many ways to reach the needy and connect with them in the most unique way. Often time's cases of domestic abuse, infidelity and crimes of passion are brought before our council of 'big uncles' and it is our duty to help those in need of comfort, solution and direction. I particularly admire how Pastor Johnson is able to pull out any scripture in the Bible to buttress any point and proffer a solution to any problem. The man was truly a remarkable MOG, Man of God. I was in total awe of him and most times, he serves as my confidant and best friend.

Talking of best friends, I remember Patrick and I am overwhelmed with the guilt feeling that I always have whenever I think of not being able to bring him into the fold of Pastor Johnson's Church. He is the friend whom I have relegated as one of my 'worldly' friends. As much as Pastor Johnson frowns upon our friendship I cannot let go of him or give up on him. He is the brother I never had. I do not have the heart to do so. Our lives are so intertwined. We work in the same establishment and live in the same private estate in Lekki. Side by side, we have grown in friendship and our families are close too. Like me he had also married and has two children who are so close with my son that you would think that they were siblings. The other snag is that Foluke disapproves of him in a way that I have not quite understood. This leaves me in a quagmire of sort whenever it comes to Patrick.

But there are some joys in my life and that is to truly give back to the society in my anonymous ways through Pastor Johnson. My regular donations are not publicized and he assures me that my contributions are well spent in taking care of the needy and the result can be attested to the large population of congregants.

I could not wait to get behind my office desk the next day to garner all the information I could about Omolola through her firm Williams and Abbot Legal practitioners. She was one woman who seemed to have dropped from the face of the earth for me until now. I needed to know why she betrayed me the way that she did. Was that the only reason? I asked myself for the tenth time today. From Wikipedia I get the information available to the public on her and her firm but not quite the information that I was looking for. For instance who is she married to? Did she ever think of me? Did she ever love me? And was our love worth just the Two Million naira that she sold it for? I have come to realize that that amount was and is probably hard to refuse but she sold out to my father. By blackmailing him? I could not believe that she could have been so despicable and conniving. As I thought of this a new wave of anger that I had not felt in years rose up within me and I had to physically restrain myself from giving way to the rage within. I had wanted to marry her, I remembered. I almost blurted it out that night when I held her in my arms in the afterglow of making love to her, but foolishly I had forgotten the ring back in my office and so I left her that night at her apartment without proposing because I needed to set the mood right. Rushing back there the next day I had met her absence and had called several times on the mobile satellite phone which had gone unanswered. And not so long afterwards my whole life had changed.

Dejectedly, I returned to my apartment hoping that she was waiting for me there only to meet Foluke at the parking lot of the apartment. She had seemed nervous and sad as though she had a premonition of what was happening because I had been thinking of how to break off things between us. Before I could say anything, she dropped the bombshell that she was pregnant and everything had changed. It was as though I was sucker-punched and I was stunned by the news because it felt as though I hardly knew her!

However, my first thought was Omolola. For a long time, I could not say anything, Foluke was the first to talk by asking 'Tokunbo aren't you going to say something?'

When I could find my voice I asked unsteadily "Are you sure?"

'Yes I am sure' she said. 'I have never missed my period and I took a pregnancy test this morning' she announced in a firm voice.

Just then, I saw a clear image of my father's disapproving

face and a further fragmentation of our relationship. How could I have been so careless and how could I persuade her from letting him know about this? I was thinking quickly of the next thing to do. I did not like what was happening at all I thought as I contemplated what to do. I need to wrap my head around this bombshell. Besides, I had not seen her in almost two months.

'Have you told anyone?' I asked; assuming the worst. Just before she could answer, Lawrence, my houseboy, interrupted us. So engrossed was I that I did not even notice him until he stood beside me.

'Good afternoon Sir,' he greeted me with a sort of trepidation in his voice. He must have noticed the tensed situation but he had a message to deliver "Ambassador called and asked that you should come and see him." As soon as he related the message that I had been summoned to the house, I knew I had my answer to the question that I had just asked Foluke.

After dismissing him, I turned to Foluke once again and waited for her response.

She began to shift from one foot to the other, 'Mummy saw me throwing up this morning and I think that she suspects'. She said putting the nail to the coffin. If her mother knew then her father would know and that meant that my father had known even before I did. After all, he was the one who had orchestrated this relationship.

"I cannot wait for us to tell our parents. Or are you not happy?" She asked with a cajoling looking.

Of course, I was not happy, but as she continued to look at me with such an imploring and scared look in her eyes I had to feign a smile and agree with her. I found myself cornered into saying the words that she wanted to hear 'I am glad.' As I said them they sounded very foreign to me. It was as though I was a third party to what was happening.

I knew I had to think about what to do next but the summons from my father was at the fore of my mind and I needed to know what he knew.

'Ok can we talk later I must go and see Daddy now' I told her in a calm voice as I tried to pretend with a calmness that I was far from feeling.

'Ok' she said as she made to hug me. I instantly recoiled from her embrace and when I saw the hurt in her eyes, I hastily corrected the awkwardness of the situation by enveloping her in a tight hug. I could feel her tenseness as we clung to each other and she held on to me a bit longer than I wanted.

If she noticed the lack of enthusiasm from me, she made no comment about it and I thought that she was probably too preoccupied with being pregnant to notice. As I got into my car I began to wish that it was Omolola who was pregnant for me instead.

Driving down to my fathers' house I had imagined that I would tell him all about Omolola because as it was, I could not marry Foluke when I was in love with Omolola, a woman that I had always loved and still loved. How was I going to keep this from her? I worried. Getting into my father's house, Mathew our long time steward met me at the door and ushered me into the house.

'Your father is waiting for you in his bedroom' he announced.

I thanked him as I made my way to his personal suite of the house. I always felt that this house was too big and grand for just a family of four and I often wondered what would happen when I started to have a family of my own. In the last two months since I began dating Omolola, I had imagined building a life with her here and filling this big house with children. But it seemed as though that was going to change now. Life without her was hard to imagine and I focused on thoughts of her as I reached for the door handle to my father's bedroom.

As soon as I stepped in, I could hear him talking on the telephone by his bedside. His bedroom was a grand master bedroom suite fitted with the most luxurious furniture and show piece for a man with such a taste for the finer things in life, it was a room worthy of a king. He was perched on the edge of the bed and as soon as he saw me he spoke into the mouth piece.

'Tokunbo is here' he paused for a minute while he listened to the speaker at the other end of the line. I stood before him while he looked up at me nodding to the phone. I knew better than to interrupt him and instead I focused on his portrait that stood at one corner of the room. As my eyes began to roam the room which also housed the latest Plasma TV, it was on mute with news from the American Cable news network. The weather news featuring on the huge TV had British born Femi Oke anchoring the latest weather report. I turned back to my father as I tried to decipher who was on the other end of the line. My suspicion grew from my mother to Chief Binuyo, a man whom I had met briefly and never really given much thought to until I started to date Foluke. Still I had not focused on the man until now. He was a short man who seemed to move ever so quickly and spoke with such alacrity too. Now, I was going to tell him that I had got his daughter pregnant and I did not want to marry her.

He soon ended the call and gestured for me to sit on one of the sofas in the seating area of the suite. I sat knowing that I was not going to like whatever it was that I was going to hear.

That was Chief Binuyo' he announced as soon as he sat down. My heart sank as soon as I heard this. He's told me the good news' he said somewhat expectant of a confirmation from me. I could only look at him.

'Is it true' he asked moving to the edge of his seat in a conspiracy manner?

'Yes daddy' I said miserably.

'Well it's all settled then' he said ignoring the look on my face. 'A man must take up his responsibilities for every action he has taken and I expect nothing less from you. As my son I expect you to do the right thing.' He continued as he reeled out all sorts of moralities to me.

He must have finally noticed the dejected look on my face and his voice soften a little as he asked 'Why do you look so miserable about it? Are you not going marry her?'

'I haven't proposed to her' I blurted out 'and I am not sure that I will; even if she is pregnant. Besides we only got together once!'

'Once is all it takes! No son of mine is irresponsible, you hear me!' he barked at me standing up to look down at me.

I decided that I would not be bullied into a life that I did not want. And I stood up matching him frame for frame, height for height.

'Daddy I do not love her. I am in love with someone else.' I announced in a calm voice.

'You are a fool!' He said. The vehemence in his voice shocked. 'Is it that local girl Omolola that you want to destroy your life for?'

'Don't call her that! I retorted and how do you know about Omolola?' I asked him.

'You think that you are clever; juggling two girls at a time. Nothing you do is ever hidden from me especially in this town Tokunbo!' he said lowering himself into his seat again. I am your father and it has taken me years of hard work and dedication to get to where we are today. Do you think it was all born out of being in love? You want to be rolling about with filth in the trenches abi?' He asked not quite answering my question on Omolola.

'How do you know about Omolola?' I insisted.

'The Omolola that you want to mess up your life for is not who you think she is. She is a conniving, low class, social climber who has used you to get ahead. How dare you consort with such a girl?'

I was confused by the things that he was saying and I thought that surely he was not talking about my Omolola.

'No daddy!' I interjected. 'You cannot be talking about my Omolola.'

'Your Omolola you say!' He said sardonically. 'She has sold out your love to the highest bidder oh! She came here just this morning demanding for money and I gave it to her, with the agreement that she will leave you alone and she collected it without batting an eyelid.'

'I don't believe you' I said as my heart began to beat a little faster in my chest. I felt as though a huge weight were crushing me as the cool air-conditioned air in the room seemed a little thinner. 'It is not Omolola.'

'Omolola Bailey' he filled in for me. Your friend came here to flaunt her relationship with you to me, threatening to expose you to the press, subjecting you to the scandal of dating her and impregnating Foluke at the same time. I will not have our family name smeared in the mud and so I accepted her terms. She wants money to further her education with a Masters' degree in law; isn't it?'

As soon as he said this I became convinced that it was Omolola but I still found it impossible to believe that she would approach my father to blackmail. And it seemed that I was the last to know about Foluke's pregnancy. Perhaps she was blinded by anger and chose to reveal our relationship to my father. In a haze of stupidity, I believed that she loved me for me and not for my money or my father's.

'But how did she know about Foluke and her pregnancy?' I asked in a whisper.

'You have been quite foolish my son, but I have been up all morning cleaning up your mess and now you owe me the curtsey of doing the right thing.'

'I still did not believe that it was Omolola, I must find her and clarify things for myself' I said making an attempt to get up. But my father quickly restrained and stopped me. I forbid you from going after that girl! Is it not bad enough that you would put us through the shame of consorting with a blackmailer and someone without a social standing? Sit down and stop being foolish. She's gone. Taken what she wants and gone with it. Must you ridicule us any further?'

I did not know what to say and when he felt that I had calmed down for a while, he got up and went to the drawer by the bedside and opened it. He soon came back with a cheque book and the mobile satellite phone that I had given to Omolola. He then proceeded to show me the stub of the leaf torn out of his cheque book where he had written Omolola Bailey's name and the sum of Two Million Naira. He left both items in my hands and I held on tightly to them.

'As you can see, your love was not cheap' he chuckled as I sat back into my seat totally deflated.

I could not believe that it was barely 24 hours ago that I was going to ask her to marry me and she would betray me like this? But then I could not help that fact that my bad luck and bad timing was responsible for the situation that had emerged. Perhaps if she had returned into my life before I met Foluke, I would not have been in this mess. But then the blackmailing bit was maddening to me. How dare she? And she came to my father especially when she knew of our unwholesome relationship. Somewhere at the back of my mind I knew that my father must have offered her the money or at least put the notion of it in her head. The fact that she took the money mislaid her moral compass and all the talk of having integrity was lost on me.

'Tokunbo, my son' he said in a soft and cajoling voice, 'you have been away for too long and you are so westernized that you do not know the schemes these sort of girls pull based on their poor background. They prey on your vulnerability. I know that you are hurting but let this be a lesson to you as to why the rich and the poor do not mix. The poor have nothing to lose. They are unscrupulous and disadvantaged and will always be poor by orientation and association. You cannot change who you are for them. They are opportunists. How do you think that I have been able to maintain our status as an affluent minority in this society of ours? Your ultimate act of retaining that level is to sustain it by marrying into the dominant stratum. Foluke is a good girl with a good social standing and our family ties will be further strengthened by your union which luckily has been cemented with her pregnancy. This Omolola is a trollop who cares about one thing alone and that is money.'

After a brief silence his face took on a grin and he began as though about to reveal a conspiracy theory "when you marry Foluke, you can have all the mistresses that you want; but not this social climber with an imperfect bloodline.'

I sat quietly with my thoughts and misery.

'Look you will have to cheer up and thank God that it hasn't got worse than it is.' My father said trying to pacify me.

When I could speak again I said 'I still cannot believe that it is the Omolola that I know!'

'Well that's life for you my boy, you can't and mustn't trust anyone that easily. But you will have to learn to trust again and your new lease of life will require just that.'

'Get up' he said raising me by the arm. 'Your mother will be arriving soon from Abuja and she is pretty excited at the thought of being a grandmother again.'

It was as though my life began from that moment on as things escalated very quickly and I had no control over the whirlpool of activities that happened soon after. In my anger at Omolola, I shoved all thoughts of her to the back of my mind as my heart dealt with the pain in other ways. The only person who asked me to pump some breaks unto the whole affair was my sister Tinuke; she had had her misgivings especially with the pace of things which according to her seemed very rushed. On the morning of the introduction ceremony, which was held at the Binuyo's residence, Tinuke had called me aside and advised me not to rush into the marriage even if Foluke was pregnant.

'Tokunbo can I speak to you' she asked peeking into my bed room at my personal wing of the family house.

'Come on in Sis' I waved her in; whilst I tried to button the cuff links of my traditional attire of Buba and Shokoto the Aso Oke Agbada which was laid out on the bed and my newly acquired Rolex wrist watch was in the midst of an equally expensive perfume. The coral bead necklace I was going to wear was a statement of value. Mother had purchased it from one of the royal houses on the Island. My shoes were of top quality leather.

'Toks are you sure that you want to do this?' She began.

'Come on Tinuke, I said looking at her 'is this the time to be asking me this question?'

'There is never a right time to ask this sort of question' she retorted. 'I just want to know that you are happy and not making the same mistakes like I did marrying for convenience rather than for love.'

'My dear sister, love is overrated these days' I said making light of her inquiry.

'Now you sound just like our father' she said reaching out to help me attach the cuff links to the sleeves of my Buba. I want you to know that I will support you in whatever decision you make.'

I could have told her the truth that I had buried for the past one month but the hurt in my heart wouldn't let me admit it. I was more focused on the baby Foluke was carrying and I swore to do right by my unborn child knowing that the love I had for Omolola would be found in the birth of my child and besides Foluke had been loving and submissive ever since we started preparing for our marriage. It would be mean of me not to take up my responsibility towards her.

'Thank you sis, but Foluke is a good girl and I am sure that she will make me a good wife.' In a state that I could only describe as being caught up in the celebratory mood that my parents were in, I continued to assure her that I knew what I was doing.

Tinuke held unto my face for a moment, then she pecked me on the cheek and whispered 'I wish you well my dear brother, may you be filled with a happy married life'

I was rather emotional at her display of affection for me because as we grew up there were less and less of these emotional encounters and having been divorced from her husband, Tinuke had developed an icy coldness towards my father and I had somewhat been a partaker of her frostiness.

Everything was in readiness for the ceremony ahead. The hall for the ceremony had been beautifully decorated; because the previous night we had had a mini rehearsal at my father's insistence that everything goes perfect and smoothly. The ceremonies had to take place quickly and timely before the pregnancy began to show. Of course Patrick was my best man and all the activities had commenced with my father throwing us a very lavish two day party, SUV's vehicles were given as wedding gifts and a honeymoon to the Bahamas. Patrick was aware of Foluke's pregnancy from the onset. He also met his wife Nkechi, on our train of bridesmaids. Foluke was the doting and proper wife and everyone said that we were the right fit for each other. And so I became a husband and a father all in the space of one year. But it seemed that the demons of the past was there to threaten my peace as I began to dream about Omolola shortly after my son Olatubosun was born. My inability to connect with the boy was a troubling one and I did not want to have the same unwholesome relationship that I had with my own father with my son. My saving grace was Pastor Aremu Johnson.

I must however confess that when I first met Pastor Johnson, I was not taken with him because I felt that he was a phony but then I was not the Christian that I am today. I did not know Christ like I do today. I had not yet experienced the fullness of life in Christ like I do today. I had been so immersed in the unwholesome naivety of my existence.

My inability to connect with my son shortly after his birth and the vivid and erotic dreams that I was having about Omolola was making me to distance myself from Foluke I could not tell anyone about my dreams because they were of Omolola carrying my infant son. However with Foluke the confidence I had in us had waned, it was as though she was wearing off of me and I was dissatisfied with my life and everything. It seemed that I had been living my life from a quiet desperation. That was when I began to smoke marijuana and drink heavily as the reality of my choice and inadequacies were catching up to me. I guess I was depressed. The truth of the matter was that I was angry and conflicted. I was angry at being married to Foluke even when she was the epitome of a perfect wife and a doting young mother. I knew in the depth of my heart, I knew I should be with Omolola but her betrayal had left me hurt and blindsided that I thought Foluke was the one for me. I tried to excuse my actions; after all, Foluke and I had been dating before I ran into Omolola again. I had done the next best thing so that I would not disgrace my father's name. My marriage was too young to be having problems.

Pastor Aremu Johnson's appearance in my life was timely. I had gone to the office on a Saturday morning as a getaway from my home and there had been this huge banner on the building just before the bank's complex advertising a Christian programme 'Sons and Fathers, Bridging the gap; A Sin savers Ministry'. Often times, on the streets of Lagos there were a number of Christian churches, groups and sects advertising one spiritual conference, seminar or the other. Patrick and I always had a good laugh at them. It wasn't that I was not a Christian myself but I was the once-in-a-while Sunday service attendee of the Anglican Church that my parents and I attended, mainly for the societal standing. There were issues that haunted me from time to time and I often wondered if they were not spiritual. I knew that I was not so much of a Christian like Foluke had turned out to be. I hardly went to church too except there was some grand occasions or during Easter and Christmas and New Year services.

And so it was a worthy mystery that I walked into that

gathering that day because I later became a part of his ministry. I addressed the issues troubling me; my young marriage and the overwhelming oppression of my father's influence. I felt as though the reality of my existence was based on the subject of his approval. With Pastor Johnson's guidance and ministrations on me I realized that I had been living in sin and through the love and mercy of God; I eventually came to realize the full potential of the love of God through forgiveness. It was that period that I gave my life to Christ and became a fulfilled born again Christian. Foluke's growth, firm devotion and conversion as a firebrand born again woman also brought us closer into the fold of Pastor Johnson's ministry. Perhaps it was my constant need to be with someone or having someone to lead me on that put me in the position that I found myself, my being born again had filled that void and I was convinced that that was where I was supposed to be and that was the life for me.

I must admit that I had tried searching for Omolola and had even swallowed my pride and I had gone to her apartment to look for her to make amends. I wished that I had tried to tell her what I felt those years ago because she was one woman with whom I had showed the depth of my heart. But her action when she found out about Foluke, her blackmail and the fact that her faith in me was so shallow convinced me that she was not worthy nor did I deem it fit to fight for her. And yet it seemed as though she had vanished from the face of the earth. Even her friend and roommate Abimbola had disappeared too and I had not met with any of her relatives while we dated. I had left it too late to go after her. But then I guessed the money she extorted from my father was enough to disappear with back then and so gradually I closed my heart and my life to the possibility of her. I never talked nor mentioned Omolola to anyone. Her betrayal was my burden to carry alone and I still carry it after all these years.

And now I knew I had a phone call to make. There were many unanswered questions still lurking at the back of my mind that would not quit bugging me. Omolola was an enigma to me and thoughts of her never quite left my mind and somewhere in my heart too. This admission to myself seemed to release a sort of burden within me and I am ashamed to admit that I felt a little at ease with the growing thought of what I intend to do.

I sent for Illyasu Ahmed the retired Secret Service agent that worked in the company as our head of security. He was a very discreet and competent fellow who I knew had integrity. He was a man that I could trust to carry out the task that I had in mind. Illyasu was also a friend. Even though he was a Muslim the fact that I was a born again Christian never affected my respect for him and his religion.

Illyasu had made good with his promise of getting me the information I wanted on Omolola and I was looking forward to seeing her again. Omolola had made good on her ambition to go for her masters in law, she had married a lawyer like herself and they had a son. Her husband Diepreye Williams, an indigene from the South-South of the country had named their son Olarinde, this was rather peculiar because the name was a Yoruba one and not a Bayelsa name from the culture where her husband came from. They had been separated for five years and he had remained in Port Harcourt and had even remarried. Omolola was, however, currently single but not without suitors as far as the report I received from Illyasu had read. She had lived in Port Harcourt during their marriage over twelve years ago, only relocating to Lagos after her divorce. I was happy to learn that she was single and had ended her last relationship with a widower whom she was dating just six months ago. My timing could not have been more perfect in making a comeback into her life.

Our second encounter after the arbitration with the community that her firm represented was an awkward one. Almost abandoning all my responsibilities and throwing caution to the wind, I had pursued her with such intensity, one would have thought that I was obsessed. I bombarded her with calls and text messages whenever I could. Many of them went unanswered. After the first call, she warned me to stay off her and asked that I respected her privacy. I asked my assistant to send her flowers after weeks of unanswered calls and messages. I am sure that my assistant must have wondered what was going on especially when those flowers were returned to me. I began to neglect my ties with the church and Pastor Johnson was beginning to notice. I knew that I was backsliding as I craved the excitement of her pursuit. Perhaps I was having some mid-life crisis. I was turning fifty in three years, and beginning to feel as though there was more to life that I was yet to conquer. When I opened my Bible to pray and seek guidance on the matter, I found myself in the book of Job asking God to help me in breaking down the barrier

'Lord I know that you can do anything and that your plans are unstoppable.' Job 42:2. I knew it was God's plan that I mend fences with this woman. Seeing her again must be part of his plans for me I convinced myself after all it did not look as though I was compromising my faith, Omolola was an unfinished business that I intended to see to its final conclusion there was some force out there that kept me going back to her. Whether I liked it or not she was a part of me that I could not seem to let go of. I was tired of bottling it all up and for some strange reason I found myself confiding in Illyasu.

After another rebuff from Omolola and seeing the returned bouquet of flowers on my assistant's table, it was a constant reminder of how fruitless my efforts were. I made my way to the restroom just to pour some water onto my face. I spotted Illyasu sitting by himself in an empty office and I approached him. He smiled getting up to greet me and I dismissed the gesture. The man was obviously older than me but due to my status as the Chief financial officer of the company it commanded some level of respect from him. I just could not help myself as I found myself unburdening my mind to him.

'I guess that there must be a deeper connection with this woman' he said smiling after I finished talking.

'You have some unfinished business with her, which you cannot seem to let go of'. He said looking at me like that way a father would his son.

'Why don't you try harder, you manage difficult and complex finances. Your approach should not only be emotional but calculating as well so that you will have a solution at the end of the day' he proffered. 'If it truly means that much to you, then let her know how you feel and make amends not with just words back it up with actions' he advised. 'Start by apologizing, no matter who is at fault. Be the man that you want her to know.' He advised me to write a letter to her and this had me in turmoil as to what to write in the letter. When I could, I wrote from the heart.

Dear Omolola,

It was a pleasant surprise seeing you again after all these years and I know that you must hate me for the way we left things in the past. I will like to make amends and hope that you can forgive me as God forgives us his own. I have tried to reach out to you several times and my efforts have been met with rejection and the bible says that one should not reject 'if God be for us, who can be against us? (Who can be our foe, if God is on our side?) Romans 8:31

Please do not be afraid to meet with me because 'God has not given us a spirit of fear, but of power and of love and of a sound mind.' 2 Tim 1:7

As a born again Christian, I have been blessed with the spirit of God's abundant mercy and love and I crave for your forgiveness and the opportunity to hear those words from you.

Please meet with me at your convenience.

I remain yours,

Tokunbo Taylor.

As I read and re read those few lines I hoped that it would soften her heart and that she would grant me an audience at the very least. I also expected an outright refusal but I was pleasantly surprised when she granted me an audience. She was attending a meeting on the Island and was having lunch at the Radisson hotel. I was shocked when I received her call summoning me. I immediately rescheduled all my meetings that afternoon as I hurriedly left my office for the hotel.

I met her at the lobby of the hotel where she received me with the formality of a professional colleague rather than that of an ex-lover. Even in that crowded lobby, there was this aura that I felt for her and I could not but hope that she felt the same. But what did I expect from her. She was being magnanimous by agreeing to see me and the least I could do was submit to her every request. She suggested that I pay for a room where we could have some privacy and I did not hesitate in doing so.

This meeting was to provide us with an opportunity to air the issues between us. It was a conversation eighteen years too late.

As soon as we walked into the room together my heart began to beat a little wildly. It felt as though I was facing a tribunal at which she would be both the judge and jury. I took a seat in one of the two chaise lounge chairs in the room not trusting my legs to continue to hold me up while I admired her slim form. She was dressed in a black dress that comfortably hugged her amazing figure and her hair had remained perfectly groomed in its Anita Baker cut even after a grueling busy Monday afternoon. She also had on some black suede high heeled shoes which aided her catwalk strides, as her hips moved to a rhythm of its own. This beautiful woman was making my heart do all kinds of jumps and I steadied myself as she waited for me to start.

Can I order us some drinks, I asked? My mouth was suddenly dry.

'No thank you. I just ate' she said reminding me of her lunch after her meeting at the Hotel's restaurant. 'But if you want a drink you can go ahead. It's your money' she added.

Instead I walked toward the fridge in the cabinet in the room and pulled out a bottle of water and poured myself a glass.

'How did you find out where I live' she asked me?

'I had someone look you up;' I admitted taking another sip of water.

'What else?' she asked in accusatory tone.

'I am sorry. I had to. You wouldn't return any of my calls.' The fact that I was obsessed with getting her to talk to me had completely occupied my mind for the past month that my wife Foluke had noticed and mentioned my unusual preoccupation to Pastor Johnson whom I had begun to avoid.

'I am only giving you audience because it is the Christian thing to do judging from your letter. But let us be clear, I may not be the bible verse quoting Christian like you; that does not make me any less a Christian than you. She said hotly.

For some reason, I could not think of a bible verse to counter what she said and I decided to quote from the bible in the book of Acts 2:38 'the bible says that we must turn from our sins and be baptized in the name of Jesus Christ so that our sins will be forgiven; and we will receive God's gift of the Holy Spirit.' Somehow I was not sure of her response as her face went through a transformation from bewilderment to anger.

'Cut the bullshit!' she retorted as soon as I finished talking.

"You think because you are versed in the doctrine and teachings of the bible I will cower before you? She asked as though incredulous of what she was hearing. 'Speak clearly like a man and stop hiding behind bible verses because if that is your method; forget it, it won't work on me.' And if you are such a strong born again Christian why are you here? She remained standing with hands akimbo.

'Omolola!' I blurted out 'I have to make amends with you!'

'Because the Bible says so?' She mocked me.

'Because my heart demands it' I replied calmly this time.

I saw her take a deep breath before continuing

"From the little that you know of me I have never pretended to be who I am not. She said. And the fact that I have decided to hear you out does not mean that I can forget the hurt that you caused me' she spat at me.

'But you compromised and collected my father's money in exchange for me......for us' I stammered in a bid to say something equally hurtful.

'I did not collect his money. He offered and I tore up the cheque in his face' she replied in astonishment. 'Weren't you in accord with his plans? Letting daddy do your dirty work for you!'

I was aghast "my father lied to me!' I thought; deflated

"If I could, I would make you understand that I had nothing to do with my father's shenanigans."

'And yet look at where we are almost twenty years later' she retorted.

'Please Omolola let me try to make it up to you, for our

sakes?'

She was silent.

"I wished I had confronted you instead of walking away like I did. The fact that Foluke was pregnant with your child while you were with me broke me and I didn't even know where to start from and ....even if I could." She hesitated wearily. "I wished that you had told me about her. If I had known I would have applied caution to my heart and not have to have heard it from your father." There is no us' she announced.

"Omolola, I am so sorry" I said as earnestly as I could. I loved you and I wanted to marry you, I was going to propose the night before I got the news that Foluke was pregnant.'

She turned away from me and went to stand by the tall French windows of the hotel room, wiping the tears from her eyes.

'It's too late' she murmured quietly' her body heaving as she continued to stare out of the window. There were only so much sorry' I could say.

'Not confronting you or speaking when I had to, had a profound impact on my life' she said still with her back turned to me.

I knew that I had to do something and take on this window of vulnerability that opened to me. I walked towards her and turned her to me enveloping her in a fierce embrace that had us both clutching at each other. A moment of absolute weakness soon overwhelmed me that I began to look for her face that was hidden against my chest and finding hers I took her lips and locked them with mine. As almost uncertain as the kiss began, it deepens and I began to savor the sweetness of her quivering lips. When we broke off she began to mumble in between sobs "I don't think you get it, I cannot forget the pain of your betrayal and the humiliation from your father. She broke off from my embrace and walked to where she had put her lap top and bag. 'I am not even sure why I agreed to hear you out anymore. What do you want from me? I mean do you think that you have the power to re write our lives?'

'I still want you' I said quickly answering her before the opportunity was lost again.

She gave a sardonic laugh.

'Omolola, there is a reason why I have been given this chance again,' very carefully choosing my next words 'if I still have this love in my heart to give you after all these years then it is because it has always been yours.

She did not speak directly to me.

"Tokunbo, you have a wife and son, I won't be that woman who breaks up a home.' She picked up her things and walked out of the room.

Chapter 6

But she was on my mind constantly and we began to

exchange memes and funny anecdotes on the available social media applications that we used as I tried to break down her walls. I really wanted to know what time and space between us had done to her and who she had become. Somewhere in my mind, she was a good person who I hoped had not stopped loving me. She was not on the popular Facebook app, neither was I an advent user of the many social media platforms because my wife sermonizes and demonize any and every bit of social media posts that she comes across. But I got my funny memes and pictures from a few colleagues of mine and I sent them to her constantly in a need to engage her. Over the numerous phone calls to each other, I enjoyed reminiscing with Omolola about our days together when we dated but somehow managed to leave out our break up. Every day, I sent a gift of every kind raging from flowers, stationaries and confectionaries to her. After a while she confessed how she looked forward to hearing from me daily but she was taking her time in renewing our friendship.

After a couple of months, I eventually wore her down and she agreed to a dinner date with me. I was determined to pull out the stops.

It was on another Thursday and I had dismissed my driver earlier in the day as I drove to the other side of the city, the Mainland. Omolola had certainly done well as she had bought an apartment all to herself in the Government residential area of Ikeja where many estates and high rise apartments were springing up in that part of town. It reminded me of the apartment I had bought after I moved back to the country many years ago. We had talked about living together there as soon as she found a job on the island. I remembered how we had christened the place with our lovemaking. We made love in practically every corner of that apartment. Those thoughts were always with me and they came back even stronger now that it would be the third time I was seeing her again. She was taking her time she said and she did not invite me into her house.

I had to wait for her by my car, watching her descend a short flight of stairs dressed in a simple one shoulder dark blue jumpsuit that was fashionably laced with white along the edges I began to experience a familiar feeling that has stayed buried somewhere within me threatening to manifest. As she walked towards me, even now she was still able to take my breath away every time I see her and it just amazes me how I feel so whole with her and with life.

'Nice ride" she said; a little breathless as she settled in beside me, in my dark blue Range Rover SUV

'Thanks' I said resisting all urges within me to reach for her and kiss her. I had been battling with the issue of where to go on a first date. Apart from a nice restaurant on the island there really weren't that many choices that I could think of as to where we could dine out and not run into one or two people who might know me. I had been out of the dating pool for so long I was afraid that I would come off as being dull. I had thought of dinning mid - air in a private jet that I could charter but that would be downright tacky and I dismissed the thought. But I had to switch things up because I remember how much fun Patrick and I had anytime we were away on either a cruise ship or on my father's yacht in the south of France where he had a private villa or when we went cycling together. We often tried on different adventures together when we had these brief trips without our wives and children. Those were the only times that I really felt relaxed and free. Sometimes, we would go cycling with friends in Nauders at the convergence of Austria's border with Italy and Switzerland. Even thinking about those rides re-awoke the adventurous spirit within me.

What I had in mind was probably a little tacky but I wanted to impress her badly and so I headed out of her drive way as a security guard saluted our exit.

I knew that the Lagos traffic to the Island was going to be a short ride since we would be driving against rush hour traffic; however the drive would give us some time to talk on the way and I gladly looked forward to it.

"Where are we going and why are we heading to the Island?" She asked when she noticed that I was inching slowly with the merging traffic on the Gbagada expressway bridge towards the third mainland bridge.

'Don't worry' I assured her 'we are going somewhere that I am sure you will not expect.'

"Well I guess whatever it is that you are up to will soon reveal itself. Wherever it is I have to be in bed by midnight because I have to be in court tomorrow morning." She said settling further into the car seat.

I smiled at her and she smiled back. There was so much I wanted to know about her and I doubted if one night would achieve that.

'So how old is your son?' I asked her noticing that she had temporarily shut her eyes a bit as if to avoid looking at me.

'Why do you want know about my son?' She asked giving me a measured look as though trying to figure me out. Even though Illyasu had done an extensive profile on her he had not found out much about the boy, I only knew that she had a son who was living and schooling in the United Kingdom with one of her siblings. Illyasu had not been able to find out exactly how old he was. Without waiting for me to continue she replied 'he is in his teenage years but I don't want to talk about my son or my ex-husband'. She warned looking serious.

I backed off from that topic knowing that it would be revisited at another time.

'I did come looking for you'. I blurted out surprising myself in the process.

'Really, how soon?' she asked as coldness descended, obliterating the light hearted mood that we had already established.

'Not soon enough' I admitted.

'Well I had to move on like your father advised'

'I am really sorry about that.' I said genuinely feeling sorry for her.

Most especially for the years apart from her again. There had always been a void within me that I think that only Omolola could fill. As almost blasphemous as it sounded she was beginning to somehow fill up that missing part of me which I thought that my faith would do. After meeting with her nearly two months ago in that hotel room I had thought that I would be overwhelmed with guilt especially since I could not forget how good she felt in my arms and how I wanted more from the kiss that we shared.

But the tide had been set and I was going to ride with it no matter the outcome. There was a reason our paths kept on crossing, invoking me with such spirited desire for this woman. This time around I would see it through till the end.

As we journey onwards and got onto the eleven kilometer third mainland bridge over the Lagos Lagoon, we both glance at our Alma matter, when she raised a finger pointing to the coastal shoreline of the University of Lagos.

'I remember sitting by that smelly shoreline waiting on you in my undergrad days like something from a fairy tale. I never went back there again, because I avoided passing by the shore line throughout the years I spent in that University' she said with a sad feeling of nostalgia.

I did not know what to say. Instead I picked up her hand and brought it to my lips giving it a reassuring kiss. For a moment, we locked eyes and I had to break away to concentrate on driving there was this silence between us that seemed to mend the situation.

We continued the journey talking about the current government policies and I was soon speeding through the traffic lights in Victoria Island.

When I branched off towards the commercial district she asked again 'Which restaurant are you taking me to?'

'We are not going to a restaurant I said mischievously. I am taking you somewhere that the dining experience is one that I am sure that you have never had before'

'I don't want anything so extravagant that would come off as being sleazy' she warned. I drove on smiling refusing to satisfy her curiosity. The roads were beginning to empty from the rush hour traffic and I soon approached our final destination. It was a high rise office complex newly constructed and sparsely inhabited.

Omolola could not seem to contain herself and instead she sighed in a bid to prevent herself from asking more questions. My smile continued to broaden as we took the elevator to the top of the building. I had made arrangement for us to have a private and intimate dining experience just for the two of us on the helipad of the tallest building on the Island. There was a grand piano with a pianist rendering a classical piece. We had a table with a single red rose in the center set right on the spot where a helicopter would land and a gazebo had been erected with some intertwined roses and that area housed a seasoned French chef waiting on us. He was an exclusive chef who had been specially contracted to cater to our dining experience. The set up looked impressive and I hoped that she would appreciate it. The view from the top was magnificent as a crisscross of festive lights illuminated our designated space and this set off a contrast to the lights of the metropolitan skyline, thereby complimenting the ambiance of the whole set up. The Mid-April night air was also refreshingly cool after a heat filled day.

For a moment or two, Omolola remained rooted to the spot and I eagerly looked at her for her approval or disapproval. I noticed how her eyes lingered on the small table that was set for two, I was not quite sure that she would like it.

'Wow! She exclaimed when she could finally say something. She held her purse to her chest and let out a huge breath.

'This is something! 'You did all this for me?' she asked

'Yes!' I answered. 'Do you like it?'

'I love it.' and she took my outstretched hand and walked with me to our table.

After ensuring that she was seated comfortably in her seat, I took mine and a waiter appeared as if on cue with the drinks menu. She opted for a 2007 Spring Mountain Cabernet Sauvignon and I was impressed by her choice because it was one of the finest wines on the wine list. Perhaps she knew a lot more about wines and was an expert I thought with a new found admiration.

'It is a good vintage wine with an award winning quality to it' she said looking at me as though expecting me to agree with her. 'I had it at a wine tasting event once.' She added

I was not an expert as I only relied on my taste bud to gauge its quality. Unlike my father who would go on a long speech on whatever wine he was drinking. But as I sat with her I began to wish that I knew extensively more on the sophisticated topic of wines so as to have something impressive to say to her. But I was mesmerized by the way her eyes were sparkling by the battery powered flames of the candlelight. The sky was lit with stars and we sipped our drinks while we waited for our three course meal. The chef had prepared a romantic menu for two which consisted of some stuffed Broiled Oysters, Terrine de Fois Gras, Glazed Carrots, creamy Potato-Celeriac Gratin, a juicy Filet Mignons with Bordelaise sauce and there was some Crème Brulee to cap it off.

It was a feast that certainly had a romantic edge to it and I marveled at the way she flawlessly ordered for her choice in French. The chef was equally pleased with her French and engaged her in a short discussion.

'I did not know that you speak French' I said to her as soon as the chef's back was turned on us.

She gave a coy smile and said 'oh just a little, it's a language I picked up during a short stay in Paris some years ago when my firm had a case that went on for a while' she added off handedly. 'But I am sure that your private investigator must have given you that information. How else would you know that I like French cuisine?' I smiled at her in response. Yes; Illyasu had been thorough.

'But you know what?' she said after taking another sip of her wine, 'I want to know about you.'

'What do you want to know?' I asked her in answer to her question.

'I mean everything; because you say that you are a born again Christian some might even take you to be a pastor in the making. Perhaps I should ask the question that has been bugging me' she said.

'Go on' I urged her.

She began hesitantly, 'How did an Ikoyi born, silver spooned 'The haves 'an Ajebutter' like you she gesticulated with two fingers in the air and she continued 'get entangled with these sort of people?' She asked.

'What sort of people?' I asked responding with a question of my own.

'I mean the have not's the 'Ajekpakos' she emphasized. Her meaning became clearer to me. 'I don't mean to sound conceited but it is people with either deep rooted spiritual problems or financial issues who roll around with pastors and churches and crusades. Tell me what led you to them?' She waited for me to answer her. I felt a bit uncomfortable with her questions.

I decided to be honest with her. 'A year after I married Foluke and after the birth of my son, I could not seem to connect with him and that was when Pastor Aremu Johnson came into my life, he saved me.' I said simply.

'Saved you? What do you mean he saved you, I thought that Jesus Christ was the only one who can do that and not your Pastor' she countered me.

'Well no! Come on, you know what I mean, I don't mean him in particular; he helped to set me on the path' he told me that I had to love God first and I had to make adjustments to my lifestyle in an effort to exercise my faith and strengthen it too.' I said defensively.

'Seems like quite a guy' she said dryly.

'But lately I have been feeling a little loss of some sort' I said confessing how I really felt whenever I was back to familiar grounds.

Looking very serious she asked 'So where does this leave me again?'

'Omolola this thing between us, I don't know what and where it will lead us but I want to assure you that I will see it through this time around. I affirmed. Just let me try.'

For a while she said nothing to this declaration of mine.

There were some frailties of man that had me questioning my beliefs these days I admitted to myself silently. If I could face sin and corruption every day and somehow manage to stay afloat from it then my head on affair with Omolola was an indication of just how much of a sinner I was. I hated to equate my feelings and association with Omolola as sinful because it feels right every time that I am with her, hers was completeness to my being.

'The fact that I am born again does not mean that I am blind my existence' I assured her. For some time now, I began to realize that even Pastor Johnson had taken advantage over me several times with some spiritual and emotional blackmail, whenever he wanted something. With the perfection of his game changer the subtlety of his methods were not lost on me. It just had not mattered until now, when the scales were beginning to fall upon the realization that he too is a man like me after all. A feeling of disheartenment had been slowly building in me for some time now. The last crusade he held had been themed 'Binding and casting of intergenerational transmission of Poverty.' It had felt ridiculous to me and I began to withdraw my association with his church. However I admit that I must have contributed to the change in his growth from a humble holy man of God, who had been focused more into the saving of souls for Christ than to this newly self-assured Gospel preacher, who seems to have exchanged his hope in eternal glory for material possession and the praise of men. When we first met he had been vehemently against those types of MOGs but now he has become like them and now he moves about with assistants and security escorts.

'So did you ever think of me? Her voice broke the silence.

'Constantly' I replied.

'I want to believe you' she said holding on with a penetrating gaze which was broken by the arrival of our meal.

She continued in her line of questioning as we began to eat, 'So what's the name of your church?'

'Christian Rapture Savers Church' I announced

'Sounds like a mouthful.' she said taking in a mouth full of her Fillet Mignon. 'What of your father? How is your relationship with him these days? She continued with what seemed like a cross examination.

'He is okay, I said uncomfortably reminded of her unpleasant history with him. He is retired now but we get along better these days.'

'How did you manage that? She asked.

'By being the son that he wanted me to be, even though I don't think that he even knew the kind of son he wanted me to be, because his plan was for me to follow in his footsteps and yet his path was not defined. It seemed as though he, too, was always trying to find his way.'

'Wow! That's deep' she said as soon as I finished talking.

'It hasn't been all that bad over the years now; my wife's much closer to him than I am.' I concluded hoping that she would change the line questioning.

'Yes your wife. What about her?' She asked as we continued with our meal.

'Are you sure you want me talking about her?' I asked her as this conversation had me feeling as though I was opening up Pandora's Box yet knowing that I would answer all her questions. When she said nothing, I began.

'Foluke is the typical Christian woman, pious and devoted to God, a good mother.'

What else could I say about my wife that would not make me seem less of a man in front of Omolola or anyone for that matter?

In truth, Foluke was a manipulative shrew prone to fits of rage, who over the years had mastered her craft in using the bible and her faith as a weapon of control and subjecting me to her every whim. She had an arrogant perception of how much of a deeply pious woman she was. Her prayers were as fiery as her tongue was sharp and she would attribute everything and anything to being worldly and sinful. One day her 16 year old niece Anuoluwa had once come crying to me because Foluke had seen a picture of her on one of her social media handles where Foluke had gone off the deep end by accusing the girl of being a member of the occult because she thought that Anuoluwa's picture on display reflected that of being a member of an Idolatry group just because the poor child had worn a red cap on her head. I still had the message on my phone:

'Good morning Anu,

The look in that your status photograph looks frightening, wild and dangerous. I hope that it is not what I am thinking? Hope that you are not in this colour idolatrous procedures or occultist programming? Jesus is the WAY, TRUTH and LIFE, no one goes to his father except through HIM. John 10:14, Mathew 6:33. But SEEK YE first the KINGDOM of God and Righteousness and all other things shall be added unto you. John15:5 Jesus is the Vine, we are branches, if he abides in us and we in him, we can do nothing. Philippians 4:13. I can do all things through Christ who strengthened me. Remain

RAPTUREABLE FOR CHRIST! Jesus is coming soon. JESUS LIVES. JESUS HEALS. JESUS SAVES. JESUS IS LORD. PLEASE STAY IN HIM!'

If an act as simple as wearing a red cap was seen as being idolatry then one can imagine how my life was with her. We were only intimate when she deemed it fit and that was a few times in a year. She was cleverly deceptive to the outside world. She hardly wore any jewelry or adorned herself with anything brilliant or bright least she be seen as a worldly woman. And she definitely paled in comparison to Omolola. Everyone believed that we were the happy Christian couple and for a very long time I must have been bewitched to believe that that was how a happy Christian marriage ought to be until Patrick stepped in. He showed me the way out by helping me to channel my pent up emotions somewhere else. So I picked up a hobby of bike riding. I survived her by managing to escape from all my pent up emotions and frustrations through refreshingly and invigorating mountain bike trips. It had become my one true passion and whenever I was stressed out I would jettison out of the country with or without Patrick. I had tried to introduce this to my son but he was not entirely keen on it.

It seemed that I went from one dominating parent to an equally domineering wife. She handled most of our finances investing in real estate as that was where real money was. Due to her clever and profitable investments, I left all my finances in her capable hands which she managed well from a suite in one of my father's high rise buildings.

But Omolola was not satisfied with my brief description of Foluke and she probed further.

'Surely that can't be all about your wife, telling me that she is a good Christian mother and wife, doesn't tell me much. Do you still love her?' she asked.

'I don't know any more' I confessed.

I decided to show her the text message from her niece Anuoluwa on my phone whilst explaining what led to it.

'It is hard to love someone when you are in constant fear of abusing her virtuous and delicate sensibilities.' I said while she read on.

As soon as she finished reading the text, she whistled and handed the phone back to me.

'My marriage to Foluke has not been without its challenges' I told her. 'It is hard to hold a decent conversation with her that would not resort to being castigated and without being ascribed to bible verses.' In all honesty I was weary of it.

But I was not keen on talking about my wife anymore and I tried to steer the focus on to Omolola.

'What do you do for fun? I asked her.

She giggled when she answered. 'I go for Owambe society parties with my recently reacquainted friend Abimbola.'

'Really, how is she?' I asked; surprised that they were still friends after so many years.

'She is alright, unmarried though.'

'Seems like a lot of our generation are either unmarried or divorced' I said

'Or widowed' she supplied morbidly.

We both looked on wistfully in agreement.

'But you seem very fit' she said eyeing me in a suspicious way.

I go bike riding whenever I can I admitted it to her and I began to tell stories of my many mountain bike rides.

As we were nearing the end of our meal the pianist started to play some love tunes and she began to smile at me. 'This has been a very nice night and I appreciate your effort.' There was sincerity in her voice.

'I am glad that you like it. So has it been sleazy or not sleazy?' I asked knowing what her answer would be. She smiled in response. As though on cue a woman dressed in a black evening dress approached from the exit door, began to walk towards us. She stopped by the pianist and began to serenade us with the 'La Vie En Rose'. I got up extended a hand to Omolola which she took hesitantly and moved into my arms. Soon we began to sway to the music.

'You know that you are the first girl I ever slow danced with' I murmured into her ear.

'I don't believe you!' she whispered back as the singer switched the lyrics from French to English.

I had heard the La Vie En Rose many times but I had never actually heard the lyrics the way I heard them with Omolola in my arms. 'Did I forget to say that you are even more beautiful than I remembered?' I said continuing to hold her close. Holding her so close to me made me feel so special and I wondered if she felt the same too. We continued to dance in silence and I tried as much as possible to hold myself back in check so as not to spoil a perfect evening. As the singer sang more love songs from the contemporary to our home grown genre of music, I mentally began to plan another equally satisfying date that hopefully would escalate to something more intimately physical. Because of her early schedule the next morning, the date had to come to an early end and I was sorry but hopeful.

As we took the lift down to the lobby of the Eggs Nest Building Omolola turned to me and took my face into her hands and kissed me in a way that I could only describe as promising as well as unobtainable.

She broke off and thanked me once again for such a romantic dinner. We made our way out of the lift into the car park and soon got into my vehicle.

Getting home later that night after dropping Omolola off at her home, I had a moment to myself on the drive back. This woman would make me happier than I have ever been and this time around there was no one to stop me from making her mine. I expected to be overwhelmed with a feeling of guilt in having spent such a satisfying evening with Omolola when I later peeped into Foluke's room, seeing her sleeping form on her bed cradling her bible to her chest, I realized that I had never been truly in love with Foluke, she had given me an initial feeling of stability and familiarity and that was probably why I remained married to her. As I continued to stare at her sleeping form with her scarf tightly wound against her temple, I am reminded of the morning crier who had chased me down on my first night with Omolola so many years ago when I was in the University of Lagos.

My wife was a different person now; she was completely stripped of that amazing personality that had first held me captive. Every year it seemed as though a chip of the goddess I married had fallen off and she had become this stranger who pushed me away finding solace and comfort in the loving arms of her religion. I did not feel threatened by her intensity for God rather I felt sorry for her and what it had made her and what was ahead. However I was more convinced that I could not give Omolola up this time around.

Ever since I made up my mind to reacquaint myself with Omolola I began to see things a little more clearly and in a more worldly way. Even as I began seeing it, really seeing myself and my life and not through the rose coloured frames of religious entrapment. I knew that I had been choosing what to see and what not to see. Now I could see my life from an outsider's eyes and it was not perfect it was considerably flawed I have not been the driving force of my life. This was not my plan nor was I the optimistic and carefree man who had returned on that flight from America after working on Wall Street so many years ago. Who had I become? Perhaps I will find out through Omolola. There was a reason I was drawn to her every now and again. I gently closed the door and walked towards my bedroom suite. We had not shared a room in years and this arrangement had manifested right after my daughter Niniola died. Foluke had change considerably by waking up in the middle of the night from nightmares and she would start chanting prayers in strange tongues. Pastor Johnson had not been enough for her in her strange malady. Her mother had stepped in by taking her to an evangelist, a woman known as 'Mother - in – Israel' the woman's intrusion into our lives had mandated that both mother and daughter spend some particular days in the month with her in heavy prayer sessions against the devil that was trying to destroy our home. She had tried to rope me in but I was skeptical and it was Pastor Johnson who was, able to convince me that the woman was a fraud and her acts and visions were hoaxes. I drew the line there but Foluke went along with it anyway and she moved out of our matrimonial bedroom soon after that. The truth of the matter now was that Foluke had become one dimensional with religion and had become misleading with the misappropriation of her faith.

But tonight after a rewarding date with Omolola, I am relieved that I would be sleeping alone, I went to bed happier and content than I had been in a very long time. Every moment now, my time away from Omolola was like an ache that only she could cure and my perspective had changed considerably. However I did not skip my responsibilities as a husband and as a father but I began to reduce my time with the CRS church and majorly with Pastor Aremu Johnson.

I know that he must have noticed the distance I was beginning to put up between us because his calls now went unanswered and unreturned. I was not yet ready to face him. He had an ability of knowing exactly what was wrong and I was not yet ready to share Omolola's existence with anyone.

Chapter 7

Chief Oriyomi Taylor was dying and he knew it. The pain in

his chest was becoming worse and he knew that it was just a matter of time before departing this life. Oh what a life he has had, he thought as a fit of cough threatened to consume him. He had been thinking about his life, and what he could remember of it. He felt unsatisfied with his son as he had always been. Tokunbo had refused to tow the path that he had set for him. The boy had simply remained impervious to his background and had finally seemed to find his way with his being 'born-again.' He was always trying to overcompensate by being modest. He had hoped that he would have enough balls to tow his footsteps. Rather his son had become a fire breeding prayer warrior bound to the strings of that Pastor who kept him in tow. No doubt he was a faithful husband and a family man, he hardly socialized with the crème de la crème. He did not even have a mistress. He had tried all his possible best to make him a fixture in the Lagos society but Tokunbo remained uninterested. But he knew that as sure as his blood ran in his son's veins, he would one day show his true traits as the son of Oriyomi Taylor. But now he was sad that he might not be alive to see that manifest. He was all alone in his huge mansion except for the domestic staffs that were still on his estate's payroll. His knew that even all the money in the world could not help him in this moment of vulnerability. His sins laid heavy on his mind and he began to remember things very clearly despite the pain in his chest. He looked at the detached ventilator beside him and vowed that he would rather die than to be hooked up to the machine and become a vegetable towards the end of his life.

There was a load within him that he had to unburden. His wife was in his other mansion in Abuja and could not be bothered to be here with him at his time of need. To be fair, he had not been a loyal husband but she had not lacked for anything. Now was the time to tie up all lose ends, and yet he felt powerless lying in his huge four poster bed. He pressed a buzzer, summoning his steward, Mathew, to his bedside. While he waited for the man to come he watched the replay of his life in slow motion.

He had been born and raised as a Catholic in one of the affluent homes of Lagos Island but over the years he had departed from that doctrine to a more accommodating one that was to suit his interests. He had not been particularly loyal to any Church only attending services to suit and enhance his social standing in the society in which he found himself. In his life time, he had stuck to being a Christian because it was the only religion he could relate with even if he had not been especially true to it. He had moved from being a born Catholic to a social Anglican and finally to the Christian Rapture Savers Church commonly called Rapturers because of his son and it was a new way that accommodated his excesses.

What no one knew was that he also practiced the occult too. And he had been promised long life through his membership and sacrifice. But now there was this need to go into confession as he began to remember the ordinances of his Catholic background, he found himself reciting Catholic prayers long abandoned. After all he was well versed in the Code of Canon Law which allowed for the necessity of confession and absolution of sins whether practicing or non-practice of the catholic order. There was no time like the present to request for the administration of the sacraments. Death was calling and he needed to confess. The problem now is that he hardly knew of any Catholic priest that he could send for to absolve him of the burden that lay heavy on his heart. Perhaps Pastor Aremu Johnson could recommend one priest. As soon as Mathew entered the room he sent for the MOG; Man of God.

If the world knew of the things he had done, the way he had manipulated people to suit his selfish needs, his name would be tarnished forever and his family would never forgive him. But he needed forgiveness and the road to that was through confession.

As soon as Pastor Johnson saw the Ambassador, his heart lurched in his chest as he knew that the end time was near and he had seen situations like these several times in his career. The Ambassador was not just a member of his congregation, the man was also a father figure to him and he was also Tokunbo Taylor's father.

'Daddy good afternoon' he said crouching beside the old man's bed even though there was a lounge chaise chair that he could pull up to the bedside. Ambassador Oriyomi smelt of medicine and something close to sourness and the pastor tried to avoid making a grimace.

'Ah Johnson' the old man said dramatically lifting a frail hand which had been resting on his chest for a hand shake to the pastor. 'Thank you for coming," he said in between breaths, "I need you to get me a Catholic priest, I want to go in for confession."

Pastor Johnson could not help the surprise on his face as his head jerked back in surprise.

The old man's request for a Catholic priest was a strange and unusual one. He did not even know that the man was a Catholic. He had known him to be Anglican before his conversion into his Church, The Christian Rapture Savers Church as one of its elderly members.

'Ok Sir' he said trying not to tire the old man who looked as though he were running out of time. 'Is there any other thing that you need? Perhaps I can send for Tokunbo too.' He suggested.

If the man was dying his son needed to be here too and it would give him an opportunity to see Tokunbo again, his friend had been very busy lately.

"No I just want the priest." The old man had said with firmness in his voice.

He was used to obeying the Ambassador's every wish in his hey days and the man was one of the financial strengths of his church. He would carry out the task for him without question. He got up 'Don't worry sir I will do as you have requested.'

On his way out of the palatial mansion he began to muse to himself and decided that he would try to find out what it was that the old man needed to get off his chest as secrets were leverage and key to power for him. Or perhaps he could persuade the man to tell him instead he thought, because he knew how tight lipped these Catholic priests were and getting one to indulge him the secrets of the great Ambassador Oriyomi Taylor was going to be hard if not next to the impossible. He would have to find out another way. He knew that he could not afford to get any of his junior pastors to pretend to be a Catholic priest. He continued to deliberate within himself on the drive to the nearest Catholic Parish on the Island to get a Priest that was willing to help him out with the dying man. He suddenly had an idea and he knew that he had to act fast or the chance and moment would be lost on him forever. He told his driver to stop at the biggest shopping Mall on the Island and he hurried inside to the nearest electronic store. He would get a tape recorder which he would slip into the old man's room to record his confession.

On getting to the Catholic Church in Victoria Island, he was given an immediate audience on account of his popularity on the Island and very soon was ushering a priest into his Toyota Land Cruiser jeep back to the Ambassador's residence. But of course hearing the name Ambassador Oriyomi Taylor was enough to get anyone up and running. The priest accompanying him was a Father Simon. The Priest's compassionate disposition was a little unnerving to him because of what he knew he was about to do. He just hoped that he could carry out the discrete act of planting the tape recorder without raising suspicion from this Priest. But he had to say something to the priest as the awkwardness of silence in the car was adding to his growing discomfort.

'Father Simon I was not quite sure that you would follow me immediately' he said breaking the silence. I expected some form of procedures or at least formalities.' Father Simon's expression registered that of surprise as his answer was like a reading from a textbook. 'Where there is imminent danger of death any penitent who is contrite for all his mortal sins and has the resolution to confess will be absolved and forgiven through the death and resurrection of Christ'.

'Even if he was not a practicing Catholic?" Pastor Johnson asked

"There are many ways God orchestrates timely confessions for his children" the priest replied.

Perhaps it was timely indeed for the Ambassador Pastor Johnson thought silently. But it was rather odd that none of his family members were present at his hour of need and deliverance. It made him to think about his own father. His mother had told him several years ago that his real father had died after falling off a fast moving Molue truck during his bus conductor years, on the perilous roads of Lagos, just a few months after he was born. He had been raised without a faith or religion often coasting from one religious house to the other until a neighbor of theirs who lived in the adjacent room of their 'face-me-I-face' you apartment had taken an interest in him and enfolded him into the Scripture Union society. He hated to think of his poor and under privileged beginnings. He often wondered how his life might have turned out if his biological father had been alive today. During the drive back to the Ambassador's house he wondered silently what secrets the old man had. He suspected that the Ambassador had some affiliation with the occult society and would not be surprised if the old man had some other children or families elsewhere.

Traffic soon eased a bit after the traffic light on the link bridge to Falomo, the drive to the Ikoyi mansion of the Ambassador was as quick as he had anticipated. A few minutes later they were ushered into the Ambassador's bedroom once more and this time Pastor Johnson insisted on entering first to inform and prepare the dying man for the priest. It also gave him the opportunity to plant the recording device.

As soon as the door shut behind the priest who had gone into confession with the old man, Pastor Johnson tried to call Tokunbo to inform him of the situation but was unable to reach him.

Ambassador Oriyomi Taylor did not die that day. He lived for another five days before he died in his sleep, a luxury that many before him could not afford. Pastor Johnson was not surprised when he was informed of the old man's demise. His mission had been accomplished in a most flawless manner and the information he had garnered from the old man's confession to the priest was a goldmine for him. Every time he listened to the recording he whistled under his breath at the revelation. But first things first. He had a role to play as the supporting clergyman and family friend of the bereaved.

The burial events lasted for four days. The old man was buried as an Anglican even after his absolution and confession as a Catholic. The days leading to the burial were dramatic with a whirlwind of activities which had included an extensive coverage by the press and several media houses. However, there had been a ceremony that the world was not privy to and even the press had been cleverly prevented from covering it but Pastor Johnson had known about it. The secret society that the late Ambassador belonged to had insisted on coming for him; he was after all 'one of their own'. It had been a tussle which had involved him when he stepped in to mediate between the family of the late Ambassador and the emissaries of that secret society. They had insisted on having his body and insisted that there was no negotiation about it as the man belonged to them. Eventually he had told them that the old man had been absolved of his sins having confessed to God through the Catholic Church into which he had been born. The deceased had revoked his ties with them. The White garment chiefs of the society had not been happy about the turn of things and insisted that they would carry out their own rites of passage for the late chief. One of the elders in the Taylor's family, had suggested that Tokunbo and his sister pacify them with an undisclosed amount of money. Pastor Johnson had wondered just how much the family had paid for the body to be allowed to lie in state during the wake because it was one of the practices that the secret societies had been against. Tokunbo was a mess and Pastor Johnson knew that he had to be a rock for his friend. The poor guy was conflicted and sad about the whole experience, if only he knew the true nature of his late father perhaps he would not be so empathetic. But the rites of passage had to be done. It was not a small fortune the Taylors were spending to send off the great Ambassador Chief Oriyomi Taylor. There were state governors and many foreign dignitaries in attendance. The number of Rolls Royce in attendance at the church was extremely impressive. Many of the money bags both old and new were subtly attired in attendance. It was, indeed, a roll call of who is who of the Lagos society. The bereaved looked resplendent and almost regal in their traditional attires. Tokunbo was dressed in the finest traditional outfit of 'Aso Oke' a long flowing robe of 'Agbada' and he looked slightly out of place in the folds of clothing that adorned his tall frame. Foluke, too had switched things up a bit as she had on a heavy make up on her usual make up free face. She seemed however a little lost as though she did not know what to with herself.

Pastor Johnson began to settle on a plan on how to upgrade his lifestyle now that the time had finally come with the demise of the late Ambassador. He could not wait to use the information he had, to garner more money from the Taylors and since they had more than they could spend in a life time he was determined to get his fair share. Pastor Johnson smiled inwardly as he looked from Foluke to the rest of the family as they sat demurely on the front row of the church pews listening to him as he spoke warmly of the man who lay in the coffin a few feet away. He had been given the privilege of delivering the sermon and his heart had swelled with pride knowing that he had to speak in front of many dignitaries present in the congregation. He had studiously prepared for the sermon hoping that he would be remembered for giving such a glowing yet frank eulogy of the deceased.

"What will you leave behind after you are gone?" That was the theme of his sermon and he began.

'Dearly beloved I am not going to talk about the Late Chief Oriyomi Taylor I am going to talk about you the living, because occasion such as this should be used to remind us about the need to remain faithful to God. He could see some of the congregants nodding in approval. He remembered the first sermon ever he had ever given as he mounted the pulpit and in that sermon he had begun:

'Dearly beloved the lord showed me that this Church is going to expand. Many souls shall be brought to Christ through my ministry. The sick will be healed, the blind will be able to see, the lame shall walk again the deaf and dumb will be able to hear and speak, old men shall have dreams and young men shall see visions because I was made for signs and wonders! Somebody should please shout hallelujah!' If it had been in his own church his wife and some other Faithfull's as he called his followers, would have shouted Hallelujah at his last remark. He was known as the Hallelujah master in his hey days.

But this was another kind of sermon and he continued: 'We

are not here to lament over the passing of Chief Oriyomi Taylor like the way the 'men of devout carried Stephen to his burial and made great lamentation over him in Acts 8:2 I am here to talk about you and what you will leave behind. In the book of Act 9:36 the bible tells us of Dorcas, a woman so full of good works and charitable deeds while at Joppa, she grew sick and died. The disciples washed her and placed her in an upper room. When Peter the disciple of Jesus Christ entered the room "all the widows stood by him weeping, showing him the tunics and garments which Dorcas had made while she was with them Acts 9:39 this godly woman was remembered by what she left behind. Revelation 14:13 says our works will follow us when we die, what will you leave behind when you die. We brought nothing into this world and we will certainly take nothing out of it 1 Tim. 6:7 our lord and savior Jesus asks what is a man profited if he gains the whole world and loses his soul? What will a man give in exchange for his soul?" (Matt. 16:26). Chief Oriyomi had certainly made a bargain with his he thought silently as he noticed that some of the congregants were beginning to look uncomfortable and shift in their pews. But he could not be stopped now as he was caught up in the throes of his preaching. He continued "we brought nothing into this world and it is certain that we can carry nothing out of this world 1 Tim. 6:7.

What would you gain if you had the whole world? Whatever it is, it will not endure after the judgment is passed 2Peter 3:10.

Even though he had told the congregants that he was talking about them he really was talking to the deceased when he asked the next question from the scriptures he had prepared. What would you give in exchange for your soul? The bible tells us that Judas sold his for 30 pieces of silver

Matt 26: 14-16. Many Christians have sold theirs for far less my people, even more so when we deny God. Many Gospel preachers have been known to exchange their hope of eternal glory for the praise of men 2 Tim. 4:3.

'Our dearly departed father has left behind a legacy not only of material value but of impressive impact on his society through public service as a diplomat. He will be missed.'

Pastor Johnson was amused by his own hypocrisy, as he spoke glowing of the deceased, pouring all praises on a man whom during his lifetime had been consumed and intoxicated with power and was an incurable mastermind at manipulating people. He could not help but detest the man a little, yet one never spoke ill of the dead. He finished his sermon by telling the congregation "The tragedy of a man's life is not how he died but how he lived'

The Taylor's family would need him even more than ever now, he thought arrogantly as he asked the congregation to bow in prayer.

The past 17 years had seemed like yesterday when he became a part of the family rendering his help; prayerfully and spiritually. He would like to take credit for the stability in the lives of the Taylor family, but he doubted if that stability would outlast the man. Often times, after the death of a patriarch in the family things had a way of falling apart. This family could be no exception. As devastated as Tokunbo was upon learning of his father's connection with the occult society he had managed to contain himself in the bizarre situation in which the revelation had thrust him. The dead man's vainglory had also put the family in such a position with the Anglican Church and it had been up to Pastor Johnson who had cleverly interposed his presence so that the Anglican Church did not catch a whiff of the underlining issues affecting the burial proceedings. But then the Anglican Church had also been adequately compensated by the Taylor's family with a huge donation running into millions of naira to the Church for one project or another.

Pastor Johnson had been with the family every day for the past two weeks since the demise of the Ambassador and today was the highlight of the events. The ride to the cemetery was a fun fare of activities. The horse drawn carriage carrying the hearse was a spectacle in itself as it drew a lot of attention from the motorists and pedestrians in the tight city of Lagos. The final place of rest for the Ambassador was the Vaults and cemetery in Ikoyi where a huge mausoleum had been built for the late chief. The deceased's wife Chief Mrs. Antonia Taylor was now crying softly as though it had just dawned on her that her partner of fifty something years was now gone from her. She was flanked on each side by her daughter and son whilst her daughter in law and the grand children stood behind her with their nannies and relatives. Some other relatives who had in the lifetime of the deceased had been beneficiaries of his various charities soon begun a slow but gradual wailing twinge on the edge of being dramatic. These same people would soon be jostling for souvenirs and party favors at the majestic reception situated at the Waterfront hall. They would also be bending their waists and spraying loose change on the popular juju musician who had been scheduled to thrill the guests and mourners.

The Anglican clergyman concluded the final prayers after each mourner had thrown their fist full of dust at the lowered coffin. Mourners began their slow depart from the edifice, leaving behind Tokunbo, Patrick and a few family members. He tried to urge Tokunbo to leave the mausoleum when suddenly there appeared a group of about six men all dressed in the burial uniform of 'Aso Ebi' of Ankara prints. They stood out because they all tied white wrappers underneath their traditional dress shirts. So the occultists were coming for their brother after all. Tokunbo began to protest vehemently when one of his elderly relatives held onto him firmly and told him in Yoruba not to interfere. Pastor Johnson knew that whatever was to happen was beyond what any of them could do anything about and he cajoled Tokunbo out of the mausoleum. For the first time in a long time Pastor Johnson and Patrick were on the same side as they both assisted Tokunbo out of the mausoleum. The white garment chiefs were free to carry out the final rites of passage for their member. As they approached the gates of the cemetery grounds with so much backward glances, a stunningly beautiful woman walked up towards Tokunbo and Pastor Johnson saw a great change come over him as he began to tremble slightly and he stopped to talk with her burying himself in a tight hug in her out stretched arms. If the circumstances had been different, Pastor Johnson would have attributed that singular encounter to something else as he felt a stirring in him by just looking at the woman. The information he had from the late Ambassador's confession however still gave him some measure of control over Tokunbo Taylor and his family, for some time now he had been sensing a change in Tokunbo as he felt his power of control over him slipping away. It was almost as though a break up was in the offing. However, it was the astonished look on Patrick's face that caused him to wonder who the woman was. The woman acknowledged Patrick with a slight nod in his direction as she hurriedly gave her condolences. They continued their walk out of the designated area of the cemetery to the car park where drummers, area boys and the occasional riff raffs and police security personnel were waiting for tips by hailing and raining accolades on them.

Chapter 8

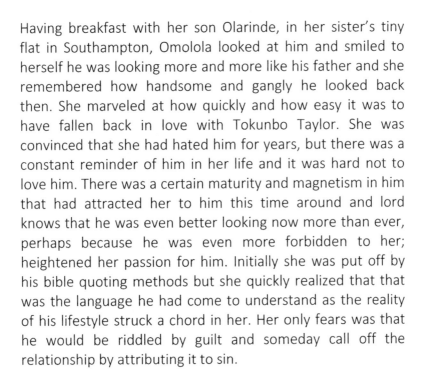

Having breakfast with her son Olarinde, in her sister's tiny flat in Southampton, Omolola looked at him and smiled to herself he was looking more and more like his father and she remembered how handsome and gangly he looked back then. She marveled at how quickly and how easy it was to have fallen back in love with Tokunbo Taylor. She was convinced that she had hated him for years, but there was a constant reminder of him in her life and it was hard not to love him. There was a certain maturity and magnetism in him that had attracted her to him this time around and lord knows that he was even better looking now more than ever, perhaps because he was even more forbidden to her; heightened her passion for him. Initially she was put off by his bible quoting methods but she quickly realized that that was the language he had come to understand as the reality of his lifestyle struck a chord in her. Her only fears was that he would be riddled by guilt and someday call off the relationship by attributing it to sin.

Her friend, Abimbola, had voiced her reservations when she learnt that Omolola was seeing Tokunbo again and had raised her objections when she told her that she had had dinner with him on a roof top.

'Look Lola,' she said when she visited Omolola in her apartment the Sunday after her date with Tokunbo.

'Is it wise to be seeing him again? Isn't he the religious type now? He is not going to leave his wife oh! How do you reconcile this kind of person with the man that was intent on destroying you? I mean this is someone who had been in your life in the past and had caused you heartbreak twice in your life Oh!' She announced after hearing the glowing details of the date night.

'I know what I am doing.' Omolola replied.

'Have you told him?' Abimbola asked

'No? Omolola said uneasily, 'I will when the time is right' she added.

'And when will that be? Just make sure that you do not tell him that Olarinde is his son when you are on top of a high rise or he might throw you off the roof this time' she added rolling her eyes at her.

Omolola rolled her eyes back at her friend and shrugged her shoulders. 'There has not been a right time yet and I know what I am doing.' she said picking up her phone that had blinked in a new message.

As she read it she began to smile and texted back a response as she giggled to herself.

Tokunbo had just asked her to accompany him to Venice, an intoxicating feeling of euphoria began to settle on her as she texted back an affirmative response.

'Look at the way you are behaving' Abimbola cautioned her, 'you are acting like a small girl don't you remember how you almost lost your mind after what that man and his father did to you?' Abimbola continued to bicker at her.

But Omolola was barely listening as she began to day dream about her upcoming trip.

'Are you listening to me?' Abimbola asked clearly annoyed at the blissful look on her friend's face.

'Of course, I hear you' she answered irritably. 'Look there is a reason why our paths keeps crossing like this, call it destiny, call it whatever you like. There is a reason why we are drawn to each other over and over again and this time there is more than just my feelings involved. Now, I have my son to think of and before you remind me that he is married and has a family of his own, let me tell you that he was mine first before anyone else. And you know what? I am going to see it through this time.'

For almost a full minute Abimbola could not say anything as she sat there looking at her friend's determined face. But Omolola was not done.

'What if something were to happen to either of us today? What happens to Olarinde? Would we not regret not seeing this relationship through? I don't have answers to any of these but I will be a damn fool if I don't take on this window of opportunity again.

'Wow, I did not know that you still felt this way about him' Abimbola replied 'I just remember all the pain and hurt that you went through all those years when we were together and the indecisions that you went through in either keeping the pregnancy or not and how hard it was for you to raise the boy on your own before Preye' came on board. I just don't want you to make another mistake with your life, I mean look at me never married still single in my forties and no kids too.

Omolola sighed and mumbled 'it is not a competition oh.' Her voice quietly resenting the way Abimbola had compared their differences.

Omolola closed her eyes betraying her embarrassment at the allusion to her friend's chronic spinsterhood; she began to remember how she had been as conflicted as she debated whether to keep the baby or not when she discovered that she was pregnant, just when she felt that she could cope with the loss of her relationship with Tokunbo Taylor. It was three months after her meeting with Ambassador Taylor that she found out that she was pregnant, bile aroused in her every time that she remembered that encounter. She had attributed the glaring symptoms that she had to the traumatic loss of her relationship. It was even more heart wrenching when she had stumbled on Tokunbo's wedding on the celebrity wedding special show that was aired on the local television station where an extensive coverage of the spectacular event had been covered. She had forced herself to watch the ceremony looking at the happy couple as they danced their way into matrimony. She had cried herself into such a state when Abimbola had discovered her all curled up in a pathetic ball. Her friend had taken pity on her as she comforted her back to life. She had watched over her like a mother hen afraid that Omolola might harm herself. Omolola had begged Abimbola not to tell her siblings about what had transpired between her and the Taylor's lest they accuse her of being overly ambitious by carrying on with the members of the elite society. Her father's disdain for the 'Ikoyi people' was an inferiority complexity that she had hated. And so when she discovered that she was pregnant with Tokunbo Taylor' s child she was torn between keeping the pregnancy as a part of having something of his in her life rather than getting rid of it in resentment for the way she had been treated and discarded by his father. She had told the world that the father of her child had died and she had given her son her father's name only changing his surname to her ex-husband's when she married him after he adopted the boy. It was when he found out the truth about the Olarinde's father through his secret birth certificate that the cracks in their relationship began which ultimately led to their divorce.

A few days ago Tokunbo had called and told her how sorry he was that he could not be with her in London at the time when she was visiting her son and how much he missed her. And now smiling at her son as he ate his breakfast she wondered how he would feel when he met his real father. She would finally have her revenge on the great Ambassador Taylor when he found out about his grandson. She was hoping to secure the future of the boy with her big reveal. But, first of all, she had to solidify her relationship with Tokunbo. She was looking forward to the weekend when she would be joining him in Venice, Italy. He had just sent her the ticket and hotel reservation and she could hardly wait to sail on the various canals and ride on the many Gondolas and the walk tours and most especially shopping from exclusive shops. Her body was awash with arousal just thinking about how they would reconnect far away from probing eyes or the negativity surrounding their relationship. She envisioned him taking her night after night in bed and on the terrace of the Bays Hotel over - looking the Grand Canal listening to the soundtrack of the lapping waves as they gently crashed on the embankment of the pier. She shivered in anticipation.

But the call she got just before she was set to go to the

airport was not the one she was expecting. Tokunbo had called informing her of the change in plans because his father Ambassador Taylor had just died! She had been crushed when she learnt of his death. She also cancelled the trip even though he had protested and asked her to take her son instead. She had refused because her son's school was in session and knowing the boy he would wear her down with questions that she was not yet ready to answer. Ambassador Taylor's death did not give her the satisfaction that she desired and she was only saddened by it for Tokunbo's sake who she knew was going to need her support emotionally and she knew that she was the only one who could give him that.

Chapter 9

'Tokunbo Taylor's life could not be controlled by his father after all' Patrick thought as he adjusted his seat in the grand dining room in the late Ambassador's mansion. When he saw Omolola at the cemetery, he knew that those two had somehow rekindled their relationship. He sighed inwardly, reminded of the role that he had played in keeping them apart. It had been at the request of the old man whom he had been subservient to. But it nagged him now that Tokunbo had managed to hook up with Omolola once more. As much as he had played his role of a devil's advocate in their relationship, it would be unsettling if Tokunbo found them apart.

He had spied for the old man and done a few unethical things that he would not want to remember again, he had also taken on the insults of not having a father figure to rely on except at whims and fancies of an arrogant socialite. Now was pay off time and Patrick listened with all eagerness for his reward.

There was an eerie silence in the room as they waited for the executor to commence. Seated in the dining room were Chief Mrs. Antonia Taylor. Patrick wondered if she was still able to carry on with younger men anymore now that she was in her early seventies. Tokunbo Taylor and his wife Foluke sat side by side holding hands like the happy couple they seemed to portray. It was, however, a surprise to him to see Tokunbo react the way he had during the burial of his father, to the white garment chiefs who had besieged the mausoleum where the late Ambassador had been laid to rest. Did he not know that his father had been a member of the occult and was he so blind to the many activities of his late father? Or perhaps he had been pretending in that holier-than-thou way of his.

Tinuke, the deceased's first born tried to mask her true feelings by faking a boredom that he knew she was far from feeling. She was alone as he suspected that she would be. There had been no love lost between the two as far as he knew. After a messy divorce from her marriage to a violent man, Tinuke had remained single, solely devoted to her daughters since her mid-thirties. She had known of her father's affiliation with the occult as her ex-husband had been a part of that sect. She was an astute business woman who lived in her father's mansion in Abuja along with her mother. There were also in attendance two relatives of the deceased, a nephew and Pastor Aremu Johnson. Patrick wondered why the Pastor was present at the reading; perhaps the old man also had a hold over the Pastor as well. The Taylors' families were a peculiar lot; he thought as he waited for the Executor to begin.

The executor, Mr. Sola Adeniyi, started by welcoming everyone and went straight to reading of the Will

This is the last will and testament of Chief Oriyomi Obatolu Taylor. . . .

'What was the old man thinking?' Patrick fumed inside him, what was a measly Ten million naira to him? His Girlfriend's apartment rent was worth that alone in a year and here he was thinking that the man had left him something worthwhile. The late Ambassador still had a way of using him even after death. The deceased had however made him the sole trustee over his grandson's inheritance of his shares, stocks and bonds. The inheritance of the grandson entrusted to him was, however, not as sizeable as what his father and Aunt got. Why the old man continued to use him this way he felt that he would never know. But he knew one thing; the man had died a billionaire and Ten Million Naira meant nothing to him and for all his years of servitude. He would overlook the insult, he consoled himself as he began to think of ways of exploiting the trust and inheritance of Bosun. The added insult was that the Pastor received the same sum too to aid his church. Did the old man really equate him with this fake Man of God? He thought as he looked into Pastor Johnson's face, trying to read any trace of self-entitlement. The man had failed to look contrite when it was announced that the sum of Ten Million Naira had been awarded to his church. There was something about him that he was yet to place about the man of God.

Pastor Johnson had put a dapper on his friendship with Tokunbo with his continuous intrusive presence. Patrick had been jealous of the way the man had tried to demote him from the position of a loyal and trusted ally to both father and son. For a man who had come from abject poverty, to mingling and rubbing shoulders with the affluent and privileged members of the Christian community and Lagos society, he felt that the man could never measure up to them. Not with his shinny suits and croc skinned shoes. He had sold himself well with his background story of having a reverent Reverend father to set him along the path to righteousness. He was sure there was much to his back story and he would find out who Pastor Johnson truly was he vowed within himself.

As he looked over at Tokunbo he thought that the only reason they were still friends was because of their jobs and the bond between their children and most especially their infrequent trips together. Whenever they were away from his family and church, Tokunbo was a different person, socially active and somewhat worldly than the self-righteous persona that he always portrayed. It was almost a Dr. Jerky and Mr. Hyde situation with him. Patrick especially enjoyed yachting on their father's vessel, wait did he just refer the deceased as his father? He wondered as he shifted uncomfortably in his chair as the executor continued with the reading of the Will. The old man had been that wealthy and it was funny that he did not have a private jet to add to the vastness of his wealth. The man had preferred the luxury of first class travel where he was pampered and adored as he lived for the power and vainglory he got from other travelers. In the past ten years as age crept up on him he could hardly leave his house and in the end he could not take any of his riches with him.

As soon as the reading of the Will was over Tokunbo came over to shake his hand.

'Patrick I am so glad that you are here. Thanks again for everything.'

"Come on, no worries man, we are practically family" he replied; wondering if he was going to bring up the topic of why he was made a trustee of his Son's inheritance.

'These past few weeks have been so stressful for me, I need a getaway soon, but work beckons you know' Tokunbo gushed on, totally avoiding the elephant in the room. Tokunbo did not need to work like a peasant like he did. He could afford to spend the rest of his life in the lap of luxury and now an added inheritance by just signing checks away.

'Did you have any idea as to why your old man left me in charge of your son's inheritance?' Patrick asked the question that was foremost on his mind.

'Look, you were like a son to him and you are like a brother to me. There is no one else in the world I would rather have entrusted such a responsibility' Tokunbo sounded sincere. 'We are family and besides who else would he have given the responsibility to if not you?'

Just then Pastor Johnson walked over and placed a hand on Tokunbo's shoulder. It almost felt territorial and the gesture greatly irritated Patrick. 'Your father was a great man and even in death his generosity goes on.'

'Thank you Pastor' Tokunbo smiled drily.

'You know Brother Tokunbo, when I met you seventeen years ago I could sense a hunger and fire in you for God. Don't let that fire die in you now' he said with its implied meaning not lost on Patrick. 'Your father is with the lord and your focus now should be with God and all that he left behind so that when it is our time there will be no more weeping and gnashing of teeth at the resurrection. He preached.

'Brother Patrick...' the Pastor began turning to him.

But Patrick cut him short. "No, no, it's just Patrick!" Pastor Johnson smiled ignoring the indulgent jab and continued 'our late father has placed a huge responsibility on you and I pray that God will grant you his grace and mercy to be able to carry out the task efficiently and effectively.

'Thank you!' He replied dryly still detesting the man's intrusion. The pastor was as greedy as they come Patrick thought even after his inheritance of Ten Million, he was still looking forward to his further exploitation of Tokunbo Taylor. He wondered what it was about this fake MOG that had Tokunbo so susceptible to him.

I will soon be taking my leave' Pastor Johnson said still resting his hand on Tokunbo's shoulder. Tokunbo turned and shook the Pastor's hand and thanked him again for being there. Patrick watched the two men, bemused. His gaze trailed Pastor Johnson as he walked towards Foluke who was standing wrapped in her thoughts.

Chapter 10

Omolola had barely settled at her desk when Endurance, her assistant, called her on her desk line to tell her that a Mrs. Foluke Taylor was waiting to meet with her. For a moment, her heart lurched in her chest and she swallowed nervously before responding into the mouth piece of the phone. 'Give me five minutes then send her in.'

Omolola got up from her seat and swept a quick look at her office as though looking for an exit. She knew that nothing good was going to come out of this unscheduled visit from Tokunbo's wife. A feeling of unease began to settle on her as she brushed her shirt into place. She quickly checked her face in her small compact mirror that she brought out from her bag and tried to calm herself.

'You got this' she said to herself as she closed the compact case and returned it into her bag. After all, she has not slept with Tokunbo yet and she was not guilty of anything the woman might want to accuse her of, she consoled herself. As she waited for the fire spitting, Christian slayer to enter her office, Omolola began a mental defense of any accusation from the woman.

But it was a totally different person who walked into her office ushered by Endurance. Foluke was not what she was expecting Omolola thought as the woman greeted her warmly and politely. Had Tokunbo lied to her? She thought, as she took in Foluke's appearance. This fair - skinned classy looking woman was different to the fanatical woman that

Tokunbo had described. She was impeccably dressed in a bedazzling Ankara jacket top on form fitted dark blue jeans and was carrying an authentic Hermes bag. Her hair was perfectly groomed as though she was coming straight from the salon and her perfume was somewhat intoxicating. She was immaculately made up by a makeup artist. Her presence was indeed one set out to intimidate.

Omolola received her equally courteously and waited for her to begin with the purpose of her visit as she settled into a chair

"What kind of lawyer are you? Foluke's question caught Omolola by surprise.

Excuse me? Omolola asked completely thrown off and still very much ill eased with her visitor.

'I mean what area do you specialize in?' Foluke was resolute.

'Conflict resolutions and Company Law' she answered getting a grip on her emotions now.

'Okay....' Foluke nodded.

Omolola watched her visitor intensely scrutinizing every bit and detail of her.

'I assume you know why I am here and who I am?' she asked suddenly switching from the sweet faced woman to a haughty self-assured stranger.

'I know who you are but I am afraid I don't know why you are here' Omolola said, wishing that Foluke would get to the point. She actually disliked the theatrics the woman across her was putting on and she was beginning to feel a slight sense of irritation rise in her as Foluke took her time in making her point.

Foluke was gradually enjoying the discomfort in Omolola as she observed what affect her presence was having on her.

'I'm sure you know my husband Tokunbo Taylor!' she taunted her.

Omolola knew that her response to this unpredictable woman would set off a chain of reactions either confirming her relationship with her husband or deepening the woman's suspicion.

'I am sure that you know the answer to that question' she countered in response.

'Hmmm' she responded pursing her lips and looking to her side as though consulting with an imaginary being.

When she turned her face towards Omolola once again her face had achieved a complete transformation. She gave off a derisive chuckle and her pretty face wore a sneer.

'I saw you at the cemetery.'

'Yes I was there because I had to pay my respects' Omolola replied, now ill at eased with Foluke's demeanor.

'I see, were you also a friend of my late father in law?' Foluke asked still not coming forward with her mission. The conversation was not going as she had planned. The woman before her was not making it easy for her with her cool exterior and the indirect way in which she was answering her questions. Her mind went back to when she saw Omolola at the Vaults and Garden cemetery. She had had a feeling about her, the way she stood out in the crowd of mourners and the way and manner in which she had embraced

Tokunbo, had sent some unpleasant shiver down her spine and she knew that Omolola was the one responsible for the change in her husband. But when she looked at Omolola now thinking of how to destroy this woman who had a huge power over her husband, she tried to find the words, the guts and courage to demand that she leave her husband alone for her but she was suddenly not sure if it would not backfire against her because the Ambassador who had been her back bone and support was dead and gone now. It was clear now that Omolola was a threat to her marriage she had just been living in the shadow of a dream.

'Why don't you ask me what it is that you really want to ask Mrs. Taylor?' Omolola asked cutting short Foluke's thoughts.

'I want you to stop sleeping with my husband' she announced in a clear and loud voice.

'You are wrong Foluke, Omolola answered her I am not sleeping with your husband!' she said holding back 'not yet anyway.' 'Your husband is an old friend and a business associate of mine.'

'Why are you lying?' she asked as she leaned forward to look into Omolola's eyes.

'Look I do not appreciate you coming to my office, throwing wild accusations at me, whatever your problem is, I will advise that you take it up with your husband and leave me out of it!'

Frustrated by the calm and control of Omolola's response, Foluke jumped to her feet, 'I know, I know the truth. I have evidence of your affair, receipts and tickets from your trip to Venice. Do you think that you can deny it and get away with it?'

'I don't know what you are talking about' Omolola rose from her seat to face Foluke matching her frame for frame. 'Now will you leave my office!'

'You've not heard the last of me. Consider this my first and final warning leave my husband alone!'

'Duly noted; please leave!' Omolola said calmly to the infuriated woman

Frustrated at not achieving the desired results, Foluke turned abruptly and left the office.

Omolola sat back heavily in her seat her heart steadying it's rhythm as she slowly recovered from the encounter.

She was weary with the way the Taylors were always warning her to keep away from Tokunbo. But how could Tokunbo have been so careless. If this was the way the way the relationship was going to be, she was not sure that she would be happy. Foluke was clearly not the woman Tokunbo had made her to expect. There was something very worldly and ungodly about her. She had expected her to spew some bible verses and curses on her but that had not happened and she gave off a slight chuckle at the thought. But, really, why had Tokunbo exposed her this way, he was not handling the situation as cleverly and as well as she hoped. He would have to step up his game right now and take a hard stance if he wanted to keep her. After a while she picked up her phone to call him.

'Hello Tokunbo' she said into the mouth piece when he picked up her call. He seemed to be on the road when he answered her.

'Hi dear' what's up? He asked in a pleasant voice 'I was going

Indeed, there was a humming sound in the bedroom and we both soon began to trace the source of the sound.

Because of the revelation of my father's affiliation with the brotherhood society, I did not know what to expect anymore as the humming every now and then would let off a squeaky sound. Even though, it sounded weird I realized that there was something mechanical about its rhythm and my heart slowed a bit as the realization that it was probably a mechanical device that was making the muffled humming sound. There was nothing fantastical, magical or evil about it. Although I silently recited Psalm 23 over and over again in my mind, the sound was actually coming from behind the huge portrait of my father's that hung on the wall by the seating area of the suite, as I went towards the portrait, I gently lifted it off the wall and it was to reveal a more intense sound that seemed to be coming from the wall. I tapped the wall since it was covered with wall paper and noticed how hollow it sounded. There was something behind the wall and it struck me that there must be a secret room or compartment behind his portrait.

'There is something behind this portrait' I disclosed to Matthew who looked as though he was ready to take off in flight.

'Here help me to put down this portrait' I said as we both lifted off the painting from the wall. The floor length portrait was carefully placed face down on the massive bed and we soon turned our attention to the wall with the mysterious sound.

'It sounds like a pacifier or an air compressor' Matthew said with relief in his voice.

I smiled at him as I continued to feel the wall for an entrance. There were no edges to indicate an opening and I was beginning to feel frustrated with the search for one when I kicked at the wall and a doorway gave way. The edges had been cleverly concealed by the shadow that the portrait had cast on the wall.

Inside had revealed a small cubbyhole with a small wooden stool and three boxes. There was a small portable air conditioner that was giving off the offending sound and not something sinister as imagined.

'Come on now, Matthew,' I said 'You must have known about this room.'

'I was aware of the coming and goings of your father for the past thirty years in this house Tokunbo, but this was not one of them' he said still looking bewildered.

I turned away from him as I squeezed my body into the small space. There were files and dossiers with names of people I did not know. On further inspection, the first box I pulled towards me had a label on the top which read FAMILY. My blood ran cold as I experienced a feeling that I could not describe. I was shocked and very upset that my father had files on his family.

Matthew shifted uncomfortably outside the cubbyhole as he waited to see my findings.

I put the box back and quickly read the covering on the other boxes they were labeled business and photos.

As consequence of the unpleasantness experienced during the burial with the embarrassing demands of members of the secret society, some of the servants had left the service of the house hold. I have resolved to keep my control on the affairs of the family until it was time for Bosun to take over.

'Tinuke and I will come and sort these out on Saturday' I said; pushing the boxes back to their resting place. 'Could you get me some water?' I asked the hovering man. And he turned abruptly leaving me with my findings. I needed the privacy. As soon as he departed I reached for the box labeled family once again and began to skim through its contents.

My father had a file on every one of us. He had a meticulous filling system that began in a stack and with the order of priority, starting with my mother's file which was surprisingly light, Tinuke and her ex-husband Fred, a file on me which I quickly opened. My file held copies of my birth certificate, school certificates shares and bonds, marriage certificate and copies of my international passports. He had documents on almost everything and anything. There were copies of letters sent and letters received over the years in all the files in the box. The next files were that of Patrick, Foluke and Olatubosun and my late daughter Niniola.

After perusing my own file and still in awe of all the information my father had kept on me, I was a little emotional that letters and drawings I had made and even forgotten about were kept in a folder for him as records.

Just as I was thinking about the uselessness of these documents to him now that he was dead, I tried to put the files back in the manner in which they had been found, I became clumsy in that hurried attempt and some documents fell to the floor. As I was putting them back into the box I came across a phone device and upon closer inspection I remembered; it was the mobile phone that I had given to Omolola. So my father collected this from her I wondered and just then I saw a cheque book, whose leaflets had been exhausted and its stubs detailing all recipients of the checks. Because it was the only leaflet of a used cheque book in the box I began to go through the stubs to see the recipients and two torn out pieces of paper that was carefully lodged in between two stubs fell out. Upon closer examination it was two halves of a torn cheque that had been addressed to Omolola Bailey with the sum of Two Million Naira. The cheque that my father had told me that Omolola had collected from him. Omolola had been telling the truth when she said she tore the cheque up in his face. I was beginning to think that I was about to unearth a lot of unsavory information about my father and there was no stopping me now as I began to probe further into this abyss of revelations.

I noticed that Foluke's folder seemed slightly bigger than any of ours and I saw some envelopes stickling out from her folder. I put everything aside as I opened her folder to look through it.

The first envelope was a birthday card and it was dated April 23rd 2000 that was my father's 65th birthday. I would have thought nothing of it had a small sticky note on the back with her cursive handwriting not catch my attention.

It's your birthday and I will show you a little something later to show that I care.

Happy birthday darling.

I was not sure of what to make of it as the hairs on my neck began to stand up. As I did the math up in my head I met Foluke on my father's birthday and she and him were ...... it was inconceivable and I was beginning to get a sinking feeling in the pit of my stomach. I did not even hear Matthew as he came back into the room with a tray carrying a bottle of water and a glass cup.

He took a look at my ashen face and set the tray down by the table. 'Tokunbo what is it?' he asked.

'I don't know yet' I said as I hurriedly began to skim through her folder. As I sat in that cubbyhole on a wooden stool I could not imagine how I must have looked with Matthew looking over my shoulder as I scanned through page after page looking for a doomed report of what I suspected.

The next note that I saw was in a small brown envelope where she had written a note *'He is asking for more money. I don't know how long we can keep this up. I need to speak with you about Tokunbo.'*

It was attached to a small stack of bank tellers with varying amounts, which were all payments made to a Pastor Deroju Onibonoje. After a quick mental calculations the bank slips came to a total of 4.5 Million Naira and was dated July 18th 2000 through to March 15th 2001.

I vaguely remember Pastor Deroju. He had been the Pastor of Foluke's former church before she joined me at Pastor Aremu Johnson's church. Pastor Deroju had died shortly in a car accident after she began attending the CRS. There were so many unanswered questions about Foluke and to think that I never knew of these payments and who was financing it and how come my father knew her like this. I probed further.

'What is this? I murmured forgetting that Matthew was still in the room with me. I stood up and came out of the cubby hole as it was beginning to suffocate me.

'Your father and your wife did a lot of businesses together' he volunteered looking at me as I moved to the seating area of the room, still clutching the files and folder before me. I dropped them on the coffee table and I continued to turn the pages, one after the other scanning for any information as quickly as I could.

'What kind of businesses?' I asked distractedly. There was nothing else to indicate anything further in Foluke's folder. Mathew had followed me and he stood beside me. I did not see the expression on his face because I was so absorbed in my quest to confirm what my head was telling me.

Worriedly my eyes rested on the box labeled photos and I grabbed it. As I looked through the photos that were neatly stacked along with some old Betamax and VHS tapes I began to feel light headed as each picture revealed a sinister side to what I had always suspected of my father. Many of the pictures were of the surveillance kind. There were photos from Pastor Deroju's accident, a picture of Patrick talking with some young lady that looked vaguely familiar, pictures of my mother with some young man in a salon, and finally a young looking photo of Foluke sitting on my father's lap in the private room of the CUE club, a private men's club, of which he had been a member. I did not want to believe it. Foluke had been a girlfriend of my father's?

As this realization sank in, so did my stomach. I did not want to think about it. A feeling of bile rose in me and I sat back heavily in the chair that I was already occupying.

'Oh my God!' I whispered. 'Foluke had been my father's girlfriend!'

'I don't believe this!' I announced forgetting once again

Mathew who picked up the picture and I was forced to lift my tortured eyes to his.

He did not seem surprised as he carefully laid the picture on to the table. There was a resigned look about him as he pulled a stool towards me and perched upon it.

'It seems that you did not know the full extent of your father's relationship with your wife?' He asked and I was too numb to answer him. It was a huge information to process.

'My father and my wife?' I asked; not expecting any response but I tried to understand the words that were coming out of my mouth.

'I thought that you knew about it?' He said in a quiet voice.

'You knew?' I asked him incredulously.

'I thought you knew' he repeated.

'Mathew what else do you know?' I implored him.

'I think that you will have to take it up with your wife, but please apply caution when doing so because your father had your best interest at heart.' He said ever so loyal to the memory of my father.

'No Mathew; tell me what you know!' I demanded of him. He said nothing.

'What is there to hide anymore?' I said angrily.

I was getting very angry, angry at finding out how my father had prevented me from marrying Omolola with his lies and now the greatest betrayal of all. Foluke the girl he had manipulated me into marrying was one of his left overs. To think that he had masterminded this deceitful union! It was an abomination before God and Man! It was unspeakable and yet I had to address the ugly situation. There must be more to it I thought as one chaotic thought clashed over another in my head. But why had he done it? Who else knew about this? I wondered, 'did my mother or my sister know?'

'I thought you knew because of your condition' he said still in that quiet voice of his.

It took a while for his words to sink in and I turned to look at him once again.

'What condition?' I asked him.

'Your father often talked about your inabilities as a man and his sacrifices and duties to help you by keeping your issues secret.'

'What are you talking about?' I asked him perplexed.

'I want to believe that I was not just a manservant to your late father but a member of this family due to your father's humility and generosity and more importantly the closeness I shared with him. I cannot say anything to tarnish his image.' He picked his words carefully.

'Look! Cut that shit out, tell me what you know!' I interrupted him rudely never minding the age difference between us. Mathew was at least twenty years older than me and this man had been devoted and loyal to my father. I knew that he had known my father the most. So he would have a lot of answers. Ever since the man died, I had been uncovering one unpleasantness or the other about him and now this? What type of person was he to have done this to me? It seemed I never really knew my father and now was the time to have all the answers. It was bad enough that I was still dealing with the stigma and embarrassment with the revelation that he had been a practicing occultist and now I find out that he had had an affair with my wife; I was not sure I could take any more nasty surprises from the man I had called my father. But I needed to know.

'I was made to believe that you had problems and you did not like women nor were you well equipped to father a child due to a childhood illness.' His voice was emotionless and he seemed to wait for my reaction.

'I don't believe this!' I said jumping to my feet. 'Jesus Christ! My father said that?' the violence in my voice must have startled Matthew.

'There is nothing wrong with me and there never has been.' I said in between breathes and disbelief. Because like every other thing I was beginning to find out about my late father, he had been a liar and a manipulator. He had lied to suit his own compulsive desires.

'I really think that you should talk it out with Pastor Johnson, especially now that your father is no more and he... he suggested timidly and well your friend Patrick too' he added after a while.

I did not even know when I began to pace back and forth in that great room. I needed to get out I thought to myself.

I soon stormed out with Matthew following me.

'Tokunbo take it easy, you hear don't go and do something that you will regret' he said following my hasty retreat from my father's bedroom.

I stopped in my tracks. What was I doing? I should find out more about this ugliness since it was bound to come out.

'I need the files' I said turning to Matthew as I made to return to the room once again. My heart was pounding in my chest as a thick cloud of vile emotions engulfed me. I pushed open the door to the room that my father had once occupied. There were so many questions and thoughts running through my head and I was hardly aware of what I was doing. I picked up the box labeled family and pointed to the one labeled photos and asked Matthew to pick it up and follow me out of the room. As soon as I emerged from the house my driver immediately brought my Range Rover to the front of the door way and I dumped the box on the car seat. I turned to collect the other box and hurriedly put that one too beside me and I climbed in after them.

'Tokunbo please!' Matthew said as he held on to the door of the SUV, 'Be calm. Don't do anything silly, please' he said pleading with me the way a parent might to a child.

'I need to go' I said pulling the door of the vehicle away from his firm hold.

As soon as I slammed shut the door, I announced calmly to my driver.' Take me to the office now.'

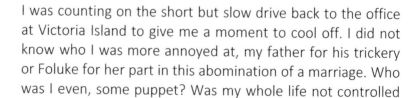

I was counting on the short but slow drive back to the office at Victoria Island to give me a moment to cool off. I did not know who I was more annoyed at, my father for his trickery or Foluke for her part in this abomination of a marriage. Who was I even, some puppet? Was my whole life not controlled by a masterful puppeteer, who I could not even accuse or fight with anymore because his death had robbed me of that chance? To think that I had cried and mourned him when he died and buried him with the love of a son in my heart? A man who tried to justify his indiscretions by implying that I was gay and impotent? It was fruitless thinking and allowing such hatred in me. But Foluke, the miserable bitch! Like a willing Jezebel she had tricked me into marrying her and I had believed it, blinded by trust while I closed my eyes to her relationship with my father. Perhaps they had even continued under my nose, I shuddered at the thought. Was Bosun really mine now that I think of it; was that the reason why I did not connect with him when he was born? 'Ah I am so dead!' I thought in anguish. And what was that, the thing that Matthew said about asking Patrick, my best friend. What did he know? And why had he hidden this from me? Was this why he did not get along with Foluke?

I needed answers and I needed them now. I picked up the folder on Foluke and made my way into my office shutting my door behind me. More often than not my office door is always open if I am alone but I needed the privacy now. I called my mother.

She picked up the phone at the second ring

'Hello dear!' she said.

'Hello Mother,' I said feeling my pulse start to rise again as I knew what I was going to ask her was going to release a barrage of questioning from her.

'How are things with you?' She asked in Yoruba and I immediately switched to Yoruba when I answered her.

'Not so good Ma,' I told her.

'Ah what is it?' she asked urgently raising her voice a little over the phone.

'I found out some things about Ambassador' I stated blandly

'What again?' There was resignation in her voice.

Did I ever have some childhood illness that affected my reproductive organs mum?' I asked

'Don't be ridiculous, of course not!' She replied. 'Where is this going, what did you find out about your father?'

This time I hesitated I was not sure that I wanted her to know how much of a sleaze her husband had been.

'I just found some pictures of him and his reference to my not been man enough like him that's all.' I said trying to down play the anguish I was really feeling.

'What kind of pictures?' She asked

'Some pictures of him and some fair skinned girls' I answered evasively.

'Yes; well those were his specs and I knew about them' she said dryly

'Look my son; don't be upset about anything your father has done to you and with his life. He is dead and accountable to his maker alone. You have your own life path to chart, so forget about anything he's said or done. He can't hurt you anymore and you are more of a man than he's ever been. You are a strong family man with strong Christian virtues.'

'So, I didn't have anything like mumps growing up?' I asked her steering her back to my previous line of question.

'No. You did not. Apart from being born slightly jaundiced and that you are aware of, there is nothing wrong with you. Remember you also had measles and childhood chicken pox like every other member of your generation. You grew up healthy and strong. Your children are an attestation to that so never doubt yourself no matter what your father must have thought of you. He was an immoral man, and like I said he cannot hurt you anymore with his sordid past.'

'Ok mum thanks, I've got to go now I will call you later' I rushed needing to end the conversation as Tinuke's call was flashing on my phone.

'Ok bye dear' she said and hung up.

'Hi! Sis' I said connecting the call to Tinuke

'Tokunbo how are you?' she asked and without waiting for a response from me she began.

'Matthew called me and told me that you discovered some things in daddy's room and they have upset you. But I thought that you were going to wait for me to come over before we start sorting his stuff out,' she accused not allowing me to get in a word.

I told her what had led to my going there and what we discovered.

'What did he have on me?' She asked.

'Doesn't look like he has anything except certificates and pictures and letters we wrote to him while we were growing up.'

'Oh I see' she said with a relief in her voice. 'So what's upsetting you?' she asked

'I found pictures of Foluke and Daddy!' I blurted out.

'No way!' She shrieked 'what kind of pictures?'

'Some documents and younger pictures of Foluke and daddy, they seemed to suggest that she was dating daddy before I met her.'

'Oh my God!' She said.' That nasty bitch! How much more of this man's transgressions are we to endure?'

'I don't know' I answered wearily' I don't know what to do right now' I said repeating myself.

'Damn! She exclaimed again 'Tokunbo just breathe ok?' I can catch an evening flight today' I imagined her looking at her wristwatch.

'No don't bother' I protested

But she interrupted me 'I don't want you to do anything stupid. You need me around you when confronting Foluke with this.'

'She's not at home today. She's gone for her two day prayer retreat' I said remembering her encounter with Omolola this morning.

'Good that will give us enough time to mobilize on what to do' Tinuke said.

'Do you know that he also prevented me from marrying Omolola I did not know what prompted me to say this.

'Who is Omolola?' She asked 'and why have you never mentioned her?'

I completely forgot that I had never talked about Omolola to her. 'It's a long story' I said as my desk phone began to ring. I raised my head to look towards the door and remembered that I had shut the door. My assistant must have gone for lunch and forwarded my office calls to my desk. I decided to ignore it but when it rang again I told Tinuke to hold on while I took the call. It was Ikechukwu one of my colleagues who wanted to drop by to discuss some figures for the next board meeting which was due in two days and I told him to come in.

'Tinuke let me call you back later' I said. 'I am meeting with someone in a minute.'

'No! But we haven't finished now' she protested but I cut her off as soon as I heard the knock on my office door.

How I was able to keep track with the presentation from Ikechukwu and figures we discussed for the upcoming board meeting was a puzzlement to me because my mind was not there at all. As soon as he left, I headed straight for my bank. I had been having a nagging suspicion since Omolola's call about Foluke discovering the plane tickets and the hotel reservations for our cancelled trip to Venice. I know that I had purchased the tickets and hotel reservation from my private and sole account. So how did she access it? The reservation confirmation had been to my official email. Going through the accounts I discovered that within three weeks since the burial, Foluke has been transferring huge sums of monies from one account to another! Besides, there had been a huge withdrawal from our business account that she was yet to reconcile with the burial expenses. Foluke had accrued it to miscellaneous expenses. Fifty Million naira was not miscellaneous. This amount I have now traced to Pastor Johnson's account! What was going on and how come I was not receiving my usual notifications? I wondered as I waited for my account officer to return to his seat. Foluke had had a free handle on this account and I had never questioned her on the activities of the account. But now I was beginning to notice discrepancies and I suspected fraud has been perpetrated on our business account. Perhaps it was foolish of me to have given her the mandate of being a sole signatory to the account but I always received notifications on the inflow and out flow of money on that account. As for my personal account there was no doubt that Foluke must have hacked into my email or accessed my account through my phone or office laptop when I worked in my study at home during the preparations for the burial.

As soon as he brought our business account profile document I spotted the reason why I was in the dark about it. My phone number had been changed to my father's number of which she must have convinced and connived with the account officer to prevent me from receiving notifications. I kept quiet. I will deal with this banker later in my own way. Right now I had an appointment with my man of God.

Chapter 12

Pastor Johnson yawned loudly as he looked at his wrist once again. He appeared bored but inwardly he was filled with an excited anticipation. He was at one of the sleekest car lofts on the Island. He was about to take final possession of the latest Mercedes Benz G-Class SUV that he had dreamed of owning ever since he heard the confession from the Ambassador. Money was pouring in from every coffer and he licked his lips in anticipation. It was his winning season and he was going to ride on this tide of good fortune that the lord had deemed fit to bless him with. The sale of the house in Ikoyi which the Ambassador had donated to his church during his life time had come together and the money belonged to him now free to do away with, in any way he pleased now that the man was dead. He had been afraid that the old man would cancel his donation but the man had been an extremely wealthy philanthropist. There was no mention of the said property during the reading of the will. During the days leading to the burial ceremony, Pastor Johnson had met with Foluke and during the first chance he got to talk with her he had told her what he knew about her and the Ambassador. Her fear had been real when he told her everything about the chief. Her support structure in the late Ambassador was dead and if she did not want her marriage and her life to be over, she would acquiesce in his demands of some Hundreds of Millions of Naira. She had expressed shock and outrage that she could not afford that money. He mentioned that he knew that she controlled the purse of Tokunbo Taylor and had some substantial shares in the Taylor dynasty, surely she could figure out something and he gave her till the day of the burial to get the money. He was glad that he did not keep girlfriends nor have any mistresses. However some women were a necessary evil and judging by Foluke and her relationship with her late father in law, he could see how easy it was to ruin a man by their power over a man's life.

Foluke had proven just how clever she was and she had paid up using the cost of settling the White garment brotherhood as a cover. She had paid her first installment of some Fifty Million Naira. A ride in the late Chief's Mercedes Benz G-Class SUV during the burial had whetted his appetite and he had wanted the ride as badly as he had never wanted anything in his life. He would ask for more he schemed as he got behind the wheels of his new ride. The latest model was over Hundred thousand Dollars and half the amount was not going to buy it unless he sold the property that was bequeathed to his Church, which he had done and got the best SUV for the best price. After all, it was his church and his to do whatever he wished. Other pastors were buying Jets and he was still stuck with house rents and all.

God was blessing him and it was time for an upgrade for his wife and their three children. He would buy a house in the choicest Estate in Lekki One and he had his eye on a luxury five bedroom house in a posh environment that was not prone to flood, as was with his present accommodation. Even with the additional Ten Million Naira that he had inherited from the late Ambassador, he still wanted more and soon too.

He would have to act fast perhaps he could add that fellow Patrick to his list of benefactors. What he knew about that guy was worth at least give or take, Tens of Millions and even more, but he had to be very careful with that one as he thought of his next strategy. The powerful roar of the Mercedes gave him such a thrill as he raced along the Lekki –

Ikoyi Link Bridge. He had finally arrived. But he was having a hard time reaching Foluke these days. Both Tokunbo and Foluke were drifting further away from him and his ministry. Tokunbo most especially and so it was a surprise when he got to his office at the church premises to find Tokunbo's dark blue Range Rover parked in front of the building at this very moment. Could it be that Foluke was here with the balance of her blackmail money? He wondered as he hurried inside the building.

He stopped as soon as he saw Tokunbo, quickly masking his disappointment.

'Good Afternoon Pastor' Tokunbo had replied with a voice that seemed forced.

'It's been quite some time since you set foot in the church oh! He said taking him by the hand. Come, let's go into my office' he said leading him to his private office.

As soon as they were both seated, Pastor Aremu Johnson began 'Ah Tokunbo before we start let us begin with a short prayer' he said still basking in the euphoria of this unscheduled visit.

'Pastor Johnson,' Tokunbo cut him short with a voice devoid of cordiality. 'You might have to save the prayer for the end of what I have to say'.

'Shuu!'Pastor Johnson was momentarily shocked but recovered soon enough to give a cheerless smile. 'Go ahead brother Tokunbo' he said reverting to the formal mood which seemed to give him a sense of authority over his members.

'What did you do with the Fifty Million Naira Foluke gave

you?' He asked deadpanned.

Pastor Johnson was dazed and for briefest of time was speechless.

Giving off a chuckle he replied:

'Ah Tokunbo, I think that you are mistaken, I did not collect any Fifty Million from your wife.'

'Come now; stop lying. I have the bank details of transfer' Tokunbo told him 'or do you think I don't know what is going on between the two of you? I took you to be a man of God for Chris - sakes!'

'Now, now Tokunbo where is this coming from?' The Pastor asked him clearly agitated with the accusation thrown at him.

'I took you to be a man of God!' He repeated 'I trusted you and yet you prey on that trust by blackmailing me?'

'Oh come off it!' He suddenly turned aggressive towards Tokunbo. Pastor Johnson was tired of the intimidation from the Taylors' family. After all their benefactor was dead and he had recently acquired newer and more powerful clientele who were even more gullible and who would lift him even higher than his present circumstances. So losing Tokunbo Taylor was not going to be a big deal. Even the Hundred Million from Foluke could be gotten elsewhere now that the cat was out of the bag. But how dare this spoilt brat insult him after all he had done for him.

'For a miserly Fifty Million naira, I saved you and your family's reputation. How else do you think that I was able to get the White Garment brothers off your backs eh?' He had something to do with her encounter with Foluke that morning. By the time she arrived at the gate to the driveway to her apartment she heaved a sigh of relief when she saw his vehicle. Tokunbo was waiting in his SUV alone. She motioned to the security guards to allow him access into the premises and when she came down from her SUV she saw him alight from his, looking quite miserable. There was no denying that something was very wrong. He looked as though he had aged considerably and his jacket hung on him like an oversized costume.

'Goodness what happened to you?' she asked not knowing if she should hug him or support his huge frame which looked as though he were ready to collapse. 'Let me lock up first' he said returning to the driver side of his SUV. 'Ok' she said looking after him with inquisitive eyes. She wondered what could have happened. A feeling of unease settled on her as she took her things into the house and collected her vehicle keys from her driver. After dismissing her driver and handing her bags to her housemaid, she turned to find Tokunbo who had now removed his jacket was climbing the small steps leading into her front doorway. 'Come on in' she urged him in to her apartment. Her apartment was cozy and stylish but Tokunbo failed to notice this as he slumped into the offered seat. 'What happened?' she asked him again.

'I don't know where to start' he appeared to be gathering his thoughts.

She sat close to him, taking his hand placing it on her lap and caressed it. Gently she told him 'You can tell me'. He looked around as if to confirm that they were alone and she assured him that they could talk. 'Come on, Tokunbo; you are scaring me. Is it me?' She asked him

'Today has been a day of horrible revelations and ugly truths. It is a day that I do not wish upon my enemy. Perhaps it is my reward for abandoning my religion. Perhaps, God is trying to show me something' he rambled on.

'Tokunbo; what are you trying to say?

'He is not my son!'

'Who told you that?' she asked.

'I was told today by those closest to me, the secret about my son.' Tears welled up in his eyes.

'They said he isn't mine.'

'But he is!' she cried along with him

'He is your son' she declared.

'How do you know?' He asked her

'How won't I know, he is also my son.'

By the time she saw the confusion in his face, she knew that he was not talking about her son Olarinde. She had been so fixated on revealing the truth about her son, that she did not know that he was not talking about Olarinde.

'What? What are you saying?' He asked her grabbing her arms.

'I am saying that Olarinde is your son.' She announced. 'That is who I thought that you were talking about. That's what I told you that I wanted to tell you this morning.'

'Are you sure?' he asked her as his listless eyes steadied.

'I have a son! He said

'I have a son!' he repeated in reaffirmation.

'You mean that your son, Olarinde is mine!' he said a little more loudly than he had intended.

'Yes he is' Omolola reconfirmed. Perplexed at his reaction to the information that had had her worried for the most part of her adult life, Omolola waited for the implication of her action to set in. But Tokunbo was basking in joy at the revelation that he was the father to her son Olarinde and his behavior both surprised and bothered her. She expected anger and shock and most importantly doubt from him but not this unprecedented behaviour.

'All day long I have been receiving one bad news after the other and the worst of it was, not knowing who I was and now you have given me the best news.'

'Tokunbo you are not making any sense' she said; not understanding what he was talking about. She stood up and was looking at him as he paced her living room stopping to pick up the framed picture of her son on the mantelpiece by the fake fire place.

'This is him?' he asked as he looked at the picture, his face going through a series of changes; they were changes that puzzled her. It was such an overwhelming but weird moment for her and she waited for him to calm down before saying anything.

'Tokunbo, you're not mad at me for keeping Olarinde a secret from you?' She asked him holding her breath for his answer. He looked at her and thought hard before he answered.

'I think I can understand your reasons'.

'What happened today, what happened to you?' she probed gently, not believing the way he was handling such life altering news.

'You know, he does look like me' he said admiring the picture of his son once more.

'Yes he is yours' she said this time more confidently as she took the picture from his hand.

'Wait here' she said as she climbed the stairs to the upper lounge leaving him to admire the other pictures of her and his son that adorned the room.

She soon returned with a huge photo album and he began to go through it page after page of pictures of the son he never knew he had. As he filled himself up with the many years of memories missed, he began to experience a sense of loss from the years that he had not been aware of Olarinde's existence and a feeling of sadness engulfed him. And Omolola took notice of it. As she closed off the last page, she carefully put the photo book aside and gently began.

'I know that you will resent me later for having kept Olarinde away from you all his life and that resentment might turn to hate sometime but I did not do it to spite you.' She said not able to look him in the eye.

'Look at me Omolola' he said; touching her face and turning it towards him. I accept you; I love you and I thank you.

As soon as he said that, Omolola's eyes filled with tears and they both clung to each other crying and soon enough their cries turned into passion as his lips found hers. As their kiss deepened, the secrets, the obstacles and the wasted years of separation between the two lovers fell away from their minds as a renewed desire was reawakened by their passion for each other. Making love to Omolola was not on his agenda but he could not resist the sweetness of her lips on his. As they both began to explore each other, he whispered in her ears 'Where is your bedroom?' She broke away and led him by the hand in response to his inquiry. Somewhere at the back of her mind she knew that he had much more to tell her but for now she was focused on the need to make love to this amazing guy who was ready to give her what she needed. Soon, they made their way up the staircase as she led him into her dimly lit, cool but spacious bedroom. They were both matured to know what they wanted and there was no need for games. Once inside, Tokunbo wasted no time in engulfing her in a fierce embrace as he continued to kiss her, tantalizing her with soft and warm kisses that made her toes curl. The way his tongue darted in her mouth, increased her already mounted desire and she moaned against his mouth. Her fingers began a journey of their own as they released the buttons on his shirt, she longed to feel his skin against her palms as she quickly helped him out of his shirt only to be hindered by the white tee shirt that stood as a barrier between her and the flesh of his torso, his hands had been equally busy as they groped and caressed every part of her, it seemed even in haste he was to be able to touch her everywhere. Her arousal tripled as he eased off every delicate piece of clothing from her body. Soon she was naked and Omolola gently pushed him into her bed and she fell on top of him. She was so turned on by the firmness of his body his muscles rippled at her touch and she went to work on him as she took control of their coupling. She began by kissing every inch of his chest playing with his taut nipples emboldened by the sexy moan that she received as reward for her actions. The lingering smell of his musky cologne gave her the boldness that she did not know that she had with her exploration and she continued to work her way downwards bringing him to the peak of release. Yet, as he held on wanting to bury himself in her she knew that she had teased him enough and she needed him to fill her with all of himself. As she came up ready to ride him he surprised her with one swift motion by turning her onto her back. From what she could see of his erect and throbbing member, she knew that she was ready to receive him into her folds but Tokunbo was not yet ready for her as he intended to repay her pleasure for pleasure.

He murmured 'my turn' as he slowly began to trail soft kisses along her shoulder down to her breasts and replayed a role that she had previously conducted on him but this time with a firm precision. She jerked in spasmodic bursts of pleasure when he continued downward finding her most intimate place bringing her unto levels of unspeakable pleasure.

By the time she was ready for him she didn't have to ask for it because he knew that she was ready to receive him in all his glory and he took her, giving her all of him. His rage and anger, his pain and joy, with every stroke he lost himself inside of Omolola. As he neared his peak, he could feel Omolola nearing hers too and he held on for as long as he could until he felt himself welcoming the sweet release in her warmth.

Chapter 14

—————————⋅◦⟨◌⟩✦⟨◌⟩◦⋅—————————

Leaving Omolola's bedside was one of the second hardest things I would ever do and in between several kisses I was finally able to tear myself away from her. Her warmth and sweetness was one that I was reluctant to let go of. I had spent an amazing night in the arms of the woman I loved and she had saved me from myself by restoring my manhood to me with the gift of a boy who I know that I would die for. My problems were waiting for me but right now they did not seem so weighty anymore. Just one night with Omolola had relieved me of that burden. My life seemed to be filled with a renewed sense of hope now.

After my meeting with Pastor Johnson I had tried to reach Patrick but his phone was engaged. Eventually I, was able to confirm from my assistant that he was in a conference call meeting with our foreign business associates. I did not feel like returning to work even though I had a lot to tidy up before the upcoming board meeting where my appointment to the board was to be confirmed. My state of mind was not the best to handle anything and I soon had my driver take me to the mainland. During the drive to Ikeja, there was considerable traffic on the roads and it gave me time to think about everything that I knew and heard about my father. I thought that I knew about all and what my father was capable of, but to be a member of an evil sect I shuddered. I then thought about myself and wondered if there was any truth in his words that I could not have fathered Bosun and that Bosun was actually my brother and not my son. It was an abomination to even speak of it and I shuddered several times. As the pain deepened in my heart, I wondered if he had ever loved me at all, was I just a pawn in his life's game of chess? My father had ruined my life with his *spirited obsession* for total control and power and I could do nothing about it. My driver must have noticed my preoccupation because he left me with my thoughts. The only interruption was to ask where we were going to on the mainland. And I gave him directions to Omolola's residence. She was still in her meeting and I had no choice but to dismiss my driver as I waited for her in my vehicle. When it seemed odd that I was parked on the street by the entrance to her block of apartments I drove down to one of the restaurants that Patrick and I used to hang out in during our younger days. It was no longer a restaurant and it was now a block of shops some of which were closed down. For the most part of that night, I drove about aimlessly until I found myself back on her street and I decided to wait for her.

How could Foluke deceive me like this; I thought. Perhaps it was my abandonment of Omolola and this was my recompense for not fighting for her? My head was about to explode with so much running through it.

Was my father right? Was I impotent and unable to father a child? I asked myself again and again. Eventually when the truth comes out, will Bosun believe me that I did know about the incestuous relationship between his mother and the man he thought was his grandfather? And will he ever recover from this trauma? How do I survive this horrible scandal? Too bad my father was not here to answer for his sins.

How was I going to handle Foluke? She had roped me into a sinful life.

As far as I was concerned, this is the end. There is no going back to what I need to do about her.

My phone rang and I saw that it was Tinuke.

'Hey Toks' she said as soon as I picked the call.

'How are you holding up?' she asked.

Ah! I sighed wearily in response.

'Don't worry I will be in Lagos tomorrow morning so we can go to Daddy's house and sort things out.' She said.

'I don't know about that' I replied, 'I've got a lot to do tomorrow. I'm preparing for the board and other important stuffs to take care. Meet me at my house instead I have the files.'

'Ok then.' Did she notice the weariness in my voice?

'Take it easy Toks' she said, confirming my suspicion.

'Thanks' I replied and ended the call.

Here I was sitting in my car waiting for Omolola instead of going home because home was an empty house. Olatubosun was away in Greece schooling in one of the finest schools there. Bosun was a late bloomer. At Seventeen he was yet to enter a university. Foluke was away on her two day spiritual mountain retreat. The only other occupants were the security guards, the cook and the steward.

I was hardly depressed but this feeling of unhappiness was threatening to drown me as I continued to sit alone with my thoughts. Who would want a man like me I thought as Omolola's text message came in apologizing for being unable to call and explaining how she was still in a meeting. Would she even want me after learning of the terrible things that my father had done. I was his offspring after all, I wondered if I had inherited any of his horrible traits.

He was such an evil man, I thought as many things began to take shape and make sense in my mind. I could not even pray about it. My revered Pastor was nothing more than a criminal, a rogue and a fraudster who used the innermost and intimate secrets of a dead man for blackmail against the living. I was conflicted as I asked why God would have allowed me to live in the midst of sin when I was faithful and devoted to him. Perhaps I had worshiped the Pastor more, and so this is my punishment. Perhaps I had not been the right Christian. These horrible revelations were enough to render anyone insane! And I felt like I was on the brink of losing my mind. When I looked at my phone I saw messages from the office and from Foluke which were nothing more than bible quotes. I ignored them all.

As I thought of what next to do, my phone rang and it was Patrick.

'Hello!'

'Hey' he said. 'You home?' He asked me.

'No.' I said 'I'm on the mainland.'

'Really at this time? Where?' he asked.

I took in a deep breath before responding. 'I am in Ikeja waiting to see Omolola.'

'Oh I see' he said as though expecting me to say more.

'You remember her now' I teased him mischievously.

'Yes I remember her' he sounded trapped.

'Toks, we have to talk' he said somewhat hesitantly

'Did Mathew call you?' I asked him.

'No, he didn't?' He responded

'Ok. We will talk tomorrow then, I've got to go now.' I said as I noticed Omolola's SUV approach her gate.

As soon as I saw her, I wanted to collapse into her arms but I needed to be strong in her presence. As I began to talk I knew I was having a hard time putting into words what I wanted to say. But when she told me that Olarinde was mine I lost it completely and my whole focus shifted completely.

Waking up entwined with her this morning felt so refreshingly good and I did not want it to end. We had taken a long shower together lathering each other lovingly and so intimately that I had taken her there again and again. Just remembering her and her lingering kisses was making me hard again and I smiled to myself as I drove homeward not minding the traffic into the island. Eventually I told her everything as we lay spent from the passion of making love to her. She did not utter a word through it all and when I was through she told me about my son and even with what she told me, I knew that there was a lot of catching up to do. She voiced her fears on telling him the truth about his father being alive after all. We both had some challenges to face and I told her that anything we would do will have to be together and will be based on the truth. She then said something which made me to think even more deeply now.

'Tokunbo despite everything that has happened, I don't want you to lose your faith in God and Jesus. God has not failed you, only man has.'

It was a very humbling moment for me and her words resonated in my head.

But she never asked me what I was going to do about Foluke.

Tinuke was on her way from the Ikeja Airport to my house in Lekki and I was hoping to get home before her. It was almost Eleven a.m. My steward had called me worried about my unusual overnight absence from the house. I told him to get some movers to come to the house. There is a lot to be done today.

Somewhere along the line I had known that sooner or later Foluke and I would go our separate ways but what I did not know was, the circumstances for that would be because of her adulterous relationship and deception with my father.

As soon as I arrived at my residence I saw that Mathew was already in the house too.

'Tokunbo thank God you are home' he exclaimed as soon as he saw me.

'Where have you been he asked?'

'I was with a friend' I said as a feeling of unease began to settle on me. As far as I was concerned he was a partaker of the ungodly relationship and his secrecy of it made him an accomplice. But then he had been loyal to my father and was probably sworn to secrecy, it would be unfair to blame on him. Still I could not help but feel cold towards him.

I wanted to discourage further conversation. But he ignored

the hint.

'I hope that you are calmer now he started.'

I pretended I did not hear him. I called Banji my steward to give him instructions on what to do.

As they stood before me, I began by asking Banji when the movers would arrive, he assured me that he had called them and they were on their way.

'I want you to start packing all of Foluke's things beginning with her room and move everything out of my house!' I announced in a calm voice. Banji looked surprised as he glanced at Mathew as though for confirmation of what he had just heard.

Mathew just bowed his head and gave a deep sigh.

'Ah, but what of Madam?' Banji asked hesitantly

'What of her?' I asked.

'Ah Oga please!' he pleaded gesturing towards Mathew as though expecting him to reason with me.

I was not angry. I was very clear as to what I wanted and needed to get done.

'Look do not question my authority. I have given instructions. You either comply or leave my household!'

He looked at Mathew again and Mathew decided to say something.

'Tokunbo please' he pleaded.

'No,' I said raising up my hand. 'It is the best thing to do at this moment' I said. I turned my back on both men and made my way up the grand staircase to my room.

I was running late for the office. I changed into a fresh shirt and a black suit and hurried out of the room. Tinuke was almost here and I decided to wait to receive her before heading to the office. I called Patrick who told me that he was in his office and I arranged to meet him at two. The stewards had gone into Foluke's room and begun packing as I had instructed. I did not care about whatever was packed as hers I needed her out of my house and out of my life. I knew that she would not take any calls nor call anyone during her two day retreat so when she arrives tomorrow she would know what has happened.

Tinuke soon arrived and her presence soon filled the empty house with her loud and boisterous personality.

'Is she back?' she asked as though preparing for a confrontation.

'So what's next?' she asked me as I looked at her with slight amusement.

'And why are you so ...?' she said unable to find the words

'So what?' I asked

'So different, unaffected even' she said when she could find the words.

I smiled and kept the information to myself. .

'Look Sis, I have a couple of things to tidy up at the office. The files are in my room, Mathew is with Banji packing her things and the movers will be here soon.' I assured her.

Patrick swallowed hard 'Tokunbo this is rather difficult to ask, but how do you know he was not lying when he said that you had had a problem.'

I took in a deep breath and said 'because I know!'

He looked at me with a strange look at my declaration. When it seemed as though he wanted me to say more I added 'Omolola reassured me.'

'How do you know that she wasn't lying?'

I was not sure I was ready to reveal the truth about my son Olarinde to anyone yet, I needed to meet him first before telling anyone about him but then I can't help that Patrick will doubt my virility 'trust me I know' I said firmly.

'Is she pregnant for you?' he asked.

I shook my head knowing that the suspense was eating at him.

'Look, I feel bad about the role I played in keeping the both of you apart, but I must tell you that Omolola demanded a payoff from your father and that was why she took off those years ago.'

'No, you are wrong and I don't blame you for thinking that way because that was the same lie that Ambassador had told me too and it made me end things with her.' I answered.

'But how do you know that she isn't lying?' he asked still in doubt.

'Omolola has no reason to lie to me. She has been very truthful with me from the beginning. I was the one who let her down when I didn't stand up for her to find out the truth.'

'But Ambassador said that she collected Two million as blackmail from him to leave you alone. He insisted.

'No, she didn't. She told me that she tore up the check in his face and I found the torn cheque yesterday along with the used up cheque book in the files he kept on all of us. For some inexplicable reason, he saved the torn up cheque.'

'He did!' Patrick's eyes widened in astonishment.

'I am truly sorry for the part I played in keeping the two of you apart.' he repeated.

'Never mind, you were just a pawn in my father's game.'

He looked relieved as I said this.

He then proceeded to tell me about his role in spying on Omolola and I during the time I dated her and just before I married Foluke. After he finished he asked 'So what are you going to do now?'

'Well my marriage is definitely over. Tinuke and the help are packing Foluke's things out, I just want her out of my life with as little noise as possible.'

'Oh Tinuke is around too?' I nodded.

'But you know going quietly is not going to happen, she won't go without a fight.' He remarked.

'It will best that she goes. What quality of life am I supposed to have with her? There are enough grounds for divorce.'

'She is going to involve Pastor Johnson and his cohorts, you know.'

'Good luck to her there. He is already blackmailing her with that information on her relationship with Ambassador.' And I proceeded to tell him about my encounter with the man.

'Wow! He exclaimed; as soon as I told him how I intended to deal with Pastor Johnson. Are you sure that you want to dabble with the occult?' He asked in a concerned voice.

'No. I won't meet with them. I will just find a way to put the word out there and they will find their way to him.'

A call on his office desk soon distracted us and he rose to answer the phone while I took out my cellphone to look at the time. We had been talking for almost two hours and I had some messages too but there was nothing particularly urgent and I waited for him to rejoin me.

When he returned to me he seemed like a new man in my eyes as though a heavy burden had been lifted off his shoulders.

It was he who restarted the conversation. 'I am glad that I am able to talk with you about this. All these while I had put up some sort of wall between us, with the heavy presence of Pastor Johnson and Foluke's deception standing there as obstacles. And I was unable to do anything about the threat to our friendship.'

I could only grunt in response. There was a nagging feeling of betrayal lurking somewhere at the back of my mind concerning Patrick but I did not want to give room to that ugly monster. Its manifestation would destroy the friendship that we had which had been largely manipulated by my late father. I needed to take control of the opportunity to redefine our friendship. He was after all my best friend and the closest thing to a brother.

I gave off a short laugh and wise – cracked; 'So my son is now my brother.'

'I am going to need some sort of deliverance when this comes out.' I stood up to leave.

'You want me to stop by the house tonight?' he asked.

'Sure.' I responded 'But Tinuke will be there and we've got stuff to sort out and talk about too.'

'Oh ok I will call you later' then he said.

I left his office and made my way back to mine. There were a few mails to respond to and I needed to finish up so that I could go back home to find out what was going on. But first I needed to hear from my sweetheart and so I placed a call to her cellphone. She answered almost immediately it rang and we caught up on each other's day. I was a little fatigued but it felt refreshingly good to speak with her. I guessed I was still basking in the euphoria of us. It was as though she had released something in me that had held me captive all these years. My heart wanted to burst in joyful exhortation I could not even describe the relief I felt knowing what news of Olarinde did to me.

I was very hungry by the time my driver pulled up to the front of my house. Tinuke was waiting for me and as soon as I settled to my meal, she joined me at the table in eager anticipation.

'Ok start talking,' she demanded,

'Can I finish my meal first?' I pleaded.

'Do you know how hard it is for me to hold myself back since yesterday? I demand that you start talking' she insisted.

In between bites, I began to talk and I started with Omolola, I told her how it all started from the University of Lagos 'Unilag' to the attempted pay off by our father. I told her about the blackmail and the money Foluke had paid the Pastor.

She hissed:

'That bitch! So it is true after all.'

'Will you let me finish I cautioned her' and I continued.

When I told her about Olarinde she exclaimed;

'Really? Can this be true? Have you met him?' She asked one question after the other.

'He is a carbon copy of me.' I said excitedly, remembering him from his photos. I have not met him yet but I will soon. Omolola has no reason to lie to me. She is the only real thing in my life right now.'

Tinuke smiled.

'You know Sis, just before I became reacquainted with Omolola, I had become disillusioned with my faith, probably because of the way Pastor Johnson had become more obsessed with money. Everything was money this, money that. He seemed to have traded his doctrine for the sole purpose of prosperity. There was no more spirituality in that church anymore. It all felt so fake and shallow and I could not put a finger on what was bothering me or why it bothered me so much.

'Well, I'm glad that your eyes are now opened and you have been released from the shackles of your blind devotion.' She began.

'You must know that this is the first time in years that I think I have held a decent conversation with you, without having to feel as though I am talking to a brick wall. I have to skirt around issues and watch my language least it offends your religious sensibilities, and without you going off all sanctimonious.'

'Wow! Was I really so closed minded?' I interjected.

'Well ...' she hesitated before continuing 'It was not all that bad but it was just a very different you. It seemed as though you were on exile from the reality of life.... You were sort of living in a bubble and I could see that you were under the manipulation and control of our Dad, Pastor Johnson and Foluke.'

'If you felt this way about me, why didn't you tell me?' I accused her!

'You are a grown ass man, I did not need to tell you how you should live your life, but Tokunbo you were not even ready to listen. Anything I would have said would have been fruitless because you believed that I was not a true believer like you. You were deaf to any opinion beyond your dogmatism.....You could not see beyond your fanaticism!'

'I am really sorry to have made you to feel that way.' I said coming to terms with what I had just heard.

'That's ok Tokunbo, you are my younger brother. I can only

hope for the best for you.' Her voice was tinged with emotion. Almost immediately, she was her boisterous self again.

'Wow! So Bosun is my brother and not my nephew, I am going to need so much therapy.' she let out with a huge sigh.

'You will need therapy?' I gasped in astonishment.

'Ok. Alright we will all need therapy' she said jokingly. Then her tone turned serious. 'I never liked her, I always felt that there was more to the way Foluke had Ambassador wrapped up.

I said nothing to this. What could I say?

My sister was not finished. 'I tried to get more information from Mathew but that man is so tight lipped, he refused to tell me anything. Even after we went to Ambassador's house where I had to have a look for myself at his private room to see what else was there. By the way we dumped her things there.'

'Dumped her things there? Why? My reaction was spontaneous.

Her retort was sharp; a veiled rebuke. 'We will not descend so low as to air our unfortunate laundry in the open. When she gets back she can go and pick her things from that abominable room.'

'I don't even want to think about how to clear up this mess that Ambassador has put us in.' I said wearily.

'Leave that to me I will not allow this to come out lest this matter become a salacious gist for some social media blogs, our privacy will be protected I will make sure of it' she continued 'let's wait to hear what she has to say for herself tomorrow.' Tinuke said, as she made to stand up from the dining table. 'Have you told Mum?' She asked turning to look at me.

'No, I don't know how.' I said truthfully.

'You should.' she said.

I shook my head 'I don't think I can.'

'You will have to Tokunbo; we can't let her find out from someone else. Perhaps you can return with me to Abuja to tell her on Sunday.'

I said nothing, thinking about the unpleasantness of that task.

'I have to be going now' she said

'Wait. Aren't you going to stay the night?' I asked

'No, I don't think so. Not in this house.' she responded.

'It's still my house' I said without enthusiasm.

'Look everything feels tainted by her.' There was sadness in her voice. 'I have a reservation at the Orient Hotel. Don't worry. I will be here first thing tomorrow morning before you set out for the office.'

As I was seeing her off, my phone beeped with text message from Patrick. He wasn't coming over anymore and wanted to know how I was holding up. I sent a quick response as soon as I waved goodbye to Tinuke.

As I went in doors I hurried to my room, it was time to say goodnight to Omolola via video call.

And now, as he continued to stare at the crumpled mass that laid at the bottom of the grand stairway, Tokunbo stood up and gently made his way down to her.

Foluke had returned unusually early from her retreat. He was knotting his tie when he heard what sounded like arguments from the gate and his heart began to quicken. He had been hoping that she would return just around noon as was her usual habit. But she was back sooner than was expected and clearly angry at being prevented from entering the premises. He was glad that the estate he lived in was a small and private one and most houses were greatly spaced out but then Foluke's voice had a way of travelling far, especially when she was agitated.

She forced her way to the entrance of the house and was now pounding at the door.

He had given firm instructions to the house helps that on no account should anyone open the door for her and he had locked the door to the main house himself keeping the keys with him in his room. The helps had remained in their quarters and kept out of sight for the ensuring altercation that they were sure, was bound to take place. Banji, however, had placed a call to Mathew and asked him to come to the Taylors residence.

Tokunbo slowly made his way down to the front of the house and braced himself for the angry confrontation that awaited him.

As soon as he opened the door Foluke barged in without even waiting for a word from him!

'What's going on? How dare you lock me out, where is Banji and Patience? She demanded.

'Banji! Patience!' She shouted for the helps.

'There is no one here for you!' Tokunbo said calmly. She stopped and looked at him in fright.

As she was about to say something he raised a finger at her and said in a steely voice. 'I am divorcing you and I want you to get out of my house.'

For a moment or two they both stood staring at each other. Tokunbo took in her somewhat different look in her oversized flowing boubou. She was not wearing a scarf as was complimentary to her usual dowdiness. She had on a perfectly groomed wig and he wondered if she was truly returning from her prayer retreat.

When his words sank in, she gave a short laugh. 'Is this some sort of a joke?'

He ignored her. 'There is nothing of yours in this house anymore. Your things have been moved and you need to leave now! He walked past her and began to climb the staircase.

By the time she regained her composure, he had reached the upper landing of the stairs and she ran after him.

'What do you mean that my things have been moved? Who moved them and how dare you? She was already in combative mood. She ran to her bed room and upon finding it empty, she gave a scream.

'Tokunbo, what have you done?' She then ran to his room to grab him as he was adjusting his tie in front of the mirror.

She descended on him grabbed at his shirt and gave him two slaps in the face. She was clearly hysterical and Tokunbo held her away from him.

'Foluke! Foluke!' he shouted pinning her arms behind her in an effort to restrain her. He looked away from her face which was terribly contorted.

'It is over! I am done with you!' He did not care about her outburst as tears of rage welled up in her eyes.

'Is it because of your whore, Omolola that you want me to leave?' she demanded in between sobs.

This time hearing Omolola's name from her got Tokunbo very angry and he grabbed her by the neck.

'Never in your life, should you mention her name!' he said in a clenched voice.

Foluke was suddenly terrified. She saw the rage in his eyes but she was not going to give up without a fight.

The devil is using you.' She said in Yoruba. 'And you have given him space and chance to use you like this!' Even though I walk through the shadow of death I will not be afraid' she began to quote from the book of Psalms in a broken voice.

Tokunbo knew that he was not a violent man and was instantly ashamed at having grabbed her by the throat. He released her and took a step back and began to unbutton his shirt.

Foluke stepped back in fear as she could not understand why he was undressing. 'What are you doing?' she asked.

Tokunbo stopped what he was doing and looked at her in disgust!

'Do you think I am a monster like my father?' He asked her. Without waiting for a response, he moved towards her once more as he continued 'Tell me is Bosun my son or my brother?'

Foluke was shocked and unable to say anything.

'Answer me now!' He bellowed as he took another step towards her. She instinctively took a step back as she began to cower in fright.

'Who told you such a thing Tokunbo?' She replied with a question of her own instead.

'Tell me the truth' he demanded; still moving with menace in his eyes.

'It's not true' she said feebly

'Do you also deny that you did not continue sleeping with my father throughout this marriage, and Niniola was not mine too?' He continued with venom in his voice.

Foluke had never seen Tokunbo like this, he seemed like a man possessed and she was deathly afraid for her life. As he moved closer she could see the veins on his neck as they throbbed in anger. She could not look away as terror consumed her. She was living out her greatest nightmare.

Instead she began to quote bible verses as though it were a talisman against this ongoing terror. 'My bible tells me that God has not given me the spirit of fear, for he is with me and I shall not be dismayed... 'Ah Mother in Israel had cautioned me oh! She warned me that the devil was out to destroy me.' she wailed.

'Oh stop that! You and I both know that you are not that deep and yours is an act of pretence' he said irritably. 'Answer my question' he shouted at her.

'It is not true' she denied vehemently.

'You may deny all you want, the evidence against you are already stacked high.' As he   changed his shirt which had become rumpled and stained from their altercation to another   one, he told the shell-shocked woman what he knew. 'From your blackmail money to Pastor Johnson to pictures and files on you from my father's love nest with you and the DNA sampling test that is ongoing he added ambitiously. 'I have all the evidence I need for a divorce. You are lucky that I am not like other men who'd have you murdered' he said calmly as he readjusted his tie.

Foluke said nothing for a moment or two and she could only look at him as reeled off what he knew.

'It was your father's idea.' It was the voice of a cornered woman, frightened but strangely steady.

'Really?' he turned to her as he bent to pick up his jacket from the edge of the bed where he had thrown it earlier when he was getting dressed before her untimely arrival.

'And now are you going to tell me that you had no part in it. The jezebel in you could not resist temptation. Is that what you are telling me?' His voice was full of contempt and it took every ounce of self-restraint in him to stop him from lunging at her.

'Look I want you out, out of this house, out of my life right now!' he said coming at her with fresh rage. It was then that Foluke saw something in his blazing eyes that gave her the fright of her life.

She backed away from the room and stopped. Making way to her room, he followed her.

'There is nothing of yours in there!' he shouted at her.

Unexpectedly, Foluke shouted back at him.

'Do you think I enjoyed it? Your father told me that you could not father a child and he had to cover your shame. That's why I did it. You could not get me pregnant.' She began in a renewed haughty manner of hers.

You can stop it right there you evil bitch! You and my father were in a relationship long before I ever came along' Weren't you, you evil woman.

'Oh I am now the evil one; after I sacrificed myself to cover up your impotence' she yelled back at him.

'Foluke shame the devil that has held you captive and set yourself free. Tell the truth. You were a runs girl who got caught up with her aristocratic boyfriend, sleeping with your father's friend! You got greedy because having my father was not enough for you had to have his son as well.'

'How dare you? How dare you Tokunbo. I am your wife I have been loyal to you and your family!'

'You are not my wife. You were my father's concubine who manipulated me into a toxic and sinful life that was perpetuated by you and your lover.'

'I am done trading words with you, leave my house! He walked past her as he made his way along the corridor that led the stairways. But Foluke soon over took him and grabbed the edge of his suit, followed him shouting.

'After eighteen years of marriage you cannot do this to me. I won't allow it!' She tried to turn him towards her but he would not budge so she manoeuvered him and stood in his path by the edge of the stairway not minding her step, the hem of her boubou tangled her restless feet. She miss-stepped and lost her balance. Tokunbo made a mad dash to catch her as she was already tumbling down the steps. The thud of her head hitting the carpeted stair-foot transfixed him and he could only watch helplessly.

───────────◦⟨⟩⟨⟩◦───────────

He could not believe what had just happened and he sat heavily at the top of the stairs. Not moving. His rage had given way to numbness and then to fear, fear of what he would find at the bottom of the stairs. He was sure that she was dead and he was terrified that he was responsible.

Patrick called him.

After telling him what had happened, he sat waiting for his friend to arrive. But before Patrick could come in, Banji opened the door and peeped into the massive foyer of the house. Seeing Foluke at the foot of the stairs where her mad tumble had come to its final resting place, he rushed to her and knelt by her still form.

This prompted a move from Tokunbo and he began a hasty descent down the stairway.

'Don't move her' he barked at the man that was crouched beside his wife.

'Mummy!' 'Mummy!' Banji cried over and over again turning her to see if there was any sign of life in her. Tokunbo was beside her now and he saw that her eyes were closed, blood was forming a pool at her temple. He yanked off the wig on her head as he told Banji to call the Hospital.

As Banji got up, Patrick opened the door took a quick look at the scene before him and gasped 'Oh my God what happened?'

'She tripped and fell from the top of the stairs' Tokunbo said as his heart began to pound loudly, as he began frantically feeling for a pulse in her. Patrick pushed him away and laid his head against the fallen woman's face.

When he raised his head he said with relief in his voice 'she is still alive' and Tokunbo heaved a huge sigh of relief.

Banji came back hovering above the two men who were on their knees with the unconscious woman. 'The Hospital says that they are sending an Ambulance'.

Patrick began to administer CPR on to the fallen woman.

Tokunbo as he sat on the floor beside them watching with unseeing eyes as Patrick continued frantic chest compressions.

Banji began to whine uncontrollably.

'Will you be quiet? Tokunbo snapped at him. The distraught man clammed up, but continued to pace and hover around the scene.

Tokunbo moved closer to see the effect Patrick's effort was having and almost immediately she began to gasp as Foluke came round.

The wail of the estate ambulance soon tore into the unnerving silence. Banji ran to the door to hurry them into the house. As the medical attendants rushed in, Tinuke followed swiftly only stopping abruptly when she saw Tokunbo seated on the floor and Foluke lying on the ground.

'What happened?' she demanded as soon as she entered the house. It seemed as though so much was happening at once and Tokunbo could only look on as the attendants strapped Foluke to the stretcher they had brought with them. They began to wheel her out of the house and into the ambulance and she asked again

'Tokunbo what happened?'

With a dazed expression he said in a quiet voice 'She tripped and fell'.

'Are you okay?' she asked turning to look at him all over as she helped him to a standing position?

'I'm fine' he said following the retreating form of his wife and the attendants out of the house to the ambulance. 'I should go with them.' he said.

'No. We will all go.' Tinuke suggested.

Tinuke took control of the situation gently steering her brother and Patrick into her car which her driver had parked behind the ambulance. Banji looked on behind them as they exited the compound, his face full of concern.

As soon as they got to the hospital she was wheeled into the intensive care unit and they were urged to wait at the waiting area specially designated for dignitaries.

As they waited Tokunbo narrated to his sister and Patrick what had ensued and his phone kept going off and on as series of messages and calls kept on trying to interrupt him. Finally when he looked at his phone he saw several missed calls and messages from his team and his assistant.

This time Patrick stood up and told him 'look Toks there is nothing you can do for her now. I suggest that you inform your team about what has happened but this is going to jeopardize your chance with the board.'

'No. I will give the presentation and come back when I'm done.' Tokunbo said gaining some level of clarity.

He was not going to lose out to a woman that was no longer worth losing anything over.

At the office he was met by his assistant who had been frantic.

As he made his way into room 234 a feeling of familiarity washed over him he braced himself for the presentation of his life.

EPILOGUE

As the Reverend preached about love deliverance and forgiveness in the Anglican Church that I now attend I look at my family as we sat in our designated and socially distanced pews reflecting on how far we have come. Through my family's tribulations a pandemic that ravaged the world, I cannot but give thanks in my heart for God's faithfulness. I am still and will always be a Christian and a believer of Christ, his love and mercy over me and my family.

It has taken me two long years after the terrible fiasco of my first marriage to my father's mistress and now ex - wife for Omolola, the woman that is meant for me, to finally say yes to my persistent need to solidify our union. Finally I am able to give her and my son my name. It had been long coming but she now bears the title Mrs. Omolola Tokunbo-Taylor. I turn my head to look at this handsome young man as he grinned at me from his seat. Olarinde Tokunbo-Taylor is going to be the best version of me. As for his uncle, his half-brother, they are best of friends. Olatubosun has shown true strength of character and maturity by accepting the news that I am his brother and not his father. He does this by showing and telling me in many ways that I would always be his father. My Omolola glows and grows in pregnancy at the age of Forty Nine and she is even more stunning every day and I cannot wait for the arrival of our baby girl.

My greatest test of faith was to forgive Foluke and cater to her disability after that horrific accident that almost took her life but took her legs instead. She lives in my father's suite in the company of her memories.

I am Tokunbo Taylor and I absolutely know who I am now.

The End.